THE PAPER PRINCESS

THE PAPER
PRINCESS

Marion Chesney

Chivers Press • Thorndike Press
Bath, England   Waterville, Maine USA

This Large Print edition is published by Chivers Press, England, and by Thorndike Press, USA.

Published in 2002 in the U.K. by arrangement with the author.

Published in 2002 in the U.S. by arrangement with Lowenstein Associates, Inc.

U.K. Hardcover ISBN 0–7540–4832–2 (Chivers Large Print)
U.K. Softcover   ISBN 0–7540–4833–0 (Camden Large Print)
U.S. Softcover   ISBN 0–7838–9626–3 (Nightingale Series Edition)

The text of this Large Print edition is unabridged.
Other aspects of the book may vary from the original edition.

Set in 16 pt. New Times Roman.

Printed in Great Britain on acid-free paper.

British Library Cataloguing in Publication Data available

Library of Congress Cataloging-in-Publication Data

Chesney, Marion.
    The paper princess / Marion Chesney.
      p.   cm.
    ISBN 0–7838–9626–3 (lg. print : sc : alk. paper)
    1. Large type books. I. Title.
    PR6053.H4535 P37 2002
    823'.914—dc21   2001051438

For Madeline Trezza,
with love.

CHAPTER ONE

'It won't happen to me. Never to me!' said Miss Felicity Channing fiercely.

'Why not?' demanded her governess, Miss Chubb. 'It's happened to your three elder sisters. Why not you?'

'I am made of sterner stuff,' said Felicity. Miss Chubb looked at her delicate charge's sensitive face and wide, vulnerable eyes and gave a cynical snort.

Both ladies were seated beside the fire in the nursery at the top of Tregarthan Castle in Cornwall. It had been an exhausting day, a day in which Felicity had watched her sister, Maria, sob her way to the altar to wed a man she barely knew.

Felicity had three elder sisters, and Maria was the last of the three to be forced by the girls' stepfather, Mr. Palfrey, into an arranged marriage. Not content with being married to one of the richest women in England, Mr. Palfrey was always on the look-out for more money to support his lavish tastes. He had married Lucy Channing, the girls' mother, when she was a pretty, young widow and the Channing girls were all still in the nursery. Felicity's mother, now Mrs. Palfrey, had been a permanent invalid for some years, allowing her husband full rein.

1

Mr. Palfrey was a thin exquisite of some forty years with a nasty waspish tongue and a determination to get his own way. His main ambition was to rid Tregarthan Castle of all his stepdaughters and then to modernize the place to suit his luxurious tastes. To that end, he had arranged marriages for each girl as she came of age. Penelope had been the first to go, wed to a baronet in Devon, then Emily to a rich merchant, and now Maria to a wealthy bishop. His aim in marrying the girls to rich men was to provide himself with the reassurance that they would make no claim on their mother's fortune. He had bullied his sick wife into making a will in which she left everything to him, having pointed out that her daughters were in no need of money. There was a 'Scotch' clause in the history of the Channings that meant the estates and fortune did not automatically become the property of the husband and could be left to the daughters, if Mrs. Palfrey chose to do so. When Mrs. Palfrey protested weakly that there was still Felicity, Mr. Palfrey replied that Felicity had turned eighteen and would soon 'be dealt with' like her sisters before her.

But Penelope, Emily, and Maria had inherited their mother's meek and biddable ways. The late Mr. Channing had been a member of the untitled aristocracy, a brave man, and a good soldier. He had also had a great zest for life, and a strong sense of humor.

Out of the four, only Felicity had inherited her father's courageous spirit.

Her elder sisters had their mother's fashionable beauty: small, straight noses; small, rosebud mouths; and dark brown hair. Felicity's dainty, elfin figure; her large greenish-gold eyes in a delicate little face; and masses of dark red hair gave her a rare elusive beauty that was all her own. Looking at her, as she sat on the other side of the nursery fire, Miss Chubb reflected that it was extremely doubtful if Mr. Palfrey knew the strength of character of the last of his stepdaughters. For Felicity was fond of her mother and did everything she diplomatically could to be quiet and biddable and not cause any of the family scenes that made her mother turn paper-white and gasp for breath.

Miss Chubb was worried about her own future. After Felicity was wed, she was expected to find another post. She could not expect a pension from Mr. Palfrey, who was tightfisted about any money that was not to be spent on his own comfort.

She knew she had little hope of finding another position. She was fifty-two, a great age in these times when the mortality rate was high. She was a squat, stocky woman with a heavy face, and large, sad, brown eyes that made her look like some old family dog.

Felicity roused herself from her reverie. 'After all, Miss Chubb,' she said, 'there is

3

surely no one left of a marriageable age in the vicinity.'

'I have heard talk,' said Miss Chubb, 'about Lord St. Dawdy.'

'I know about him. He is in his fifties and has been married twice before. Also, he was not invited to the wedding, which shows a blessed lack of interest in him.'

'He would have been invited had he not been on the Grand Tour.'

'Indeed! I thought only very young men went on the Grand Tour.'

'It is said that the baron has been several times,' said Miss Chubb.

'My stepfather does not know me very well. He will find it difficult to force me into marriage with anyone.'

Miss Chubb forbore from depressing her young friend by pointing out the obvious—that a woman did not have any say in the matter, never had, and never would.

'I would not be too nice in my choice of gentlemen,' mused Felicity, her chin on her hand. 'I must admit that neither Penelope nor Emily seems to have any complaints, and Penelope has those darling children. Children must be a great comfort.'

'Do you not have romantic dreams?' asked Miss Chubb, who had a great many herself.

'Oh, no, not I,' said Felicity with a laugh. 'I am eminently practical. But I would have freedom of choice, you know, and not be treated like some slave. I mean to have a say; neither of my three sisters ever tried saying, "No."'

'Perhaps they knew it would not have been of much use,' ventured Miss Chubb cautiously.

'Pooh! They are afraid of Mr. Palfrey. But I am not! It is early yet. Has he retired?'

'I do not think so,' said Miss Chubb. 'One of the guests at the wedding breakfast spilt wine on the dining room floor, and just before I came up to join you, he was screaming at the housemaids and saying that no one must rest until the floor was restored to its former glory.'

Felicity sighed. Due to Mr. Palfrey's finicky tastes, Tregarthan Castle was like a museum. It was not a medieval castle, but a relatively modern one, a sort of folly built in the middle of the last century by her grandfather, who had had romantic tastes. It even had a moat with a drawbridge, turrets with arrow slits, and great metal cauldrons on the battlements for pouring boiling oil down on the invading troops who had lived only in her grandfather's active imagination.

Inside, everything was polished to a high shine. Precious objects lay embedded in silk in rows of glass cases, for Mr. Palfrey was a great collector of *objets d'art*. Not a cobweb, not a speck of dust was allowed to sully any surface. The servants were overworked and consequently surly. Only this nursery up under the leads had been spared Mr. Palfrey's

5

collecting and cleaning zeal. It was cluttered with some of the furniture he considered too old-fashioned for the state rooms belowstairs, including two fine Chinese Chippendale chairs and a carved William & Mary chest.

'Let us dress up and go out,' said Felicity suddenly. Miss Chubb looked scared.

Sometimes, she and Felicity would dress up in men's clothes and ride to the nearest tavern. It was a small adventure because they usually went out when Mr. Palfrey was visiting in London and there could be no chance of their absence being noticed. The only servant in on the secret was the head groom, John Tremayne, who detested Mr. Palfrey with a passion and who only stayed on out of loyalty to the remaining Channings.

Felicity was still too young to realize it was most odd for an old and, seemingly, conventional governess to agree to such mad escapades, and did not yet even guess how very romantic and starved for adventure was poor Miss Chubb.

'Mr. Palfrey might come looking for you,' said Miss Chubb.

'To kiss me good night? You know he never pays me the slightest heed.'

'Miss Felicity, he is a fussy and ambitious man—ambitious to have the castle to himself. He will be anxious to arrange a marriage for you as soon as possible and may call you downstairs to discuss the matter. You may remember that Maria was sent for just after Emily had gone off with her new husband.'

'Yes, yes. But Maria's bishop had been selected for her some time before Emily's marriage. You must admit, there is no one left for me—thank goodness!'

'You forget Lord St. Dawdy.'

'Now, my dear Miss Chubb, the baron is abroad and he is too old even for my wicked stepfather to consider asking him to marry me, so there is no question of him sending for me. He is probably down on his hands and knees at this moment polishing the dining room floor himself.'

Miss Chubb hesitated. She thought she had overheard Mr. Palfrey saying something about the Lord St. Dawdy and Felicity. On the other hand, the baron was surely far too old. It would cause a scandal in the neighborhood if Felicity were forced to marry him, and Mr. Palfrey longed to be admired and respected by the tenants as Mr. Channing had been admired and respected. Also, she enjoyed these harmless adventures. In the last century, when Miss Chubb had been governess to a lively family of girls in Brighton, the girls had gone to assemblies dressed as men for a joke and nobody had seemed to find it shocking. But times had changed and society was more strait-laced in this second decade of the nineteenth century. But she longed to escape from the castle, just for a little.

'Perhaps it would not be noticed . . .' she started to say and was interrupted by Felicity.

'My best of governesses!' she cried. 'Hurry up! A ride across the moors is just what we need.'

Felicity and Miss Chubb had spent one wet afternoon two years before studying the old plans of the castle. They had found, to their delight, a priest's hole, albeit a fake one, the castle having been built well after the days of the Cavaliers and Roundheads, and a secret staircase. Their disguises were hidden in the priest's hole and the staircase enabled them to make their way out of the castle unobserved.

Soon, what looked to all appearances like a slim youth and a heavy, John Bull-type of gentleman slipped through the darkness of the grounds to the stables after having negotiated the moat by means of a long ladder laid across it—the one part of the adventure Miss Chubb never enjoyed because she was sure the ladder would break one dark night under her weight.

It was a November evening, but unusually balmy. It had been a warm autumn and the stunted trees on the moors were only just beginning to send the last of their scarlet and gold leaves flying down on the warm, sticky gales which blew in from the sea.

Miss Chubb was not a good horsewoman and the old, steady mare John Tremayne had found for her suited her needs, being as slow and cautious as she was herself. Felicity had a frisky little Arab mare, a dainty little creature that could fly like the wind. Miss Chubb's mount could not keep up with it, so Felicity had to content herself by riding off on long gallops on her own and then turning back to join the governess, whose horse was steadily and surely plodding sedately along the cliff path.

These little adventures had never palled, never lost their feeling of excitement, although they never entailed any real fear of discovery.

Felicity and Miss Chubb would ride to The Green Dolphin tavern, a well-appointed inn that drew people from all over because of the excellence of its food. They would drink two glasses of wine each, staying about half an hour, and then ride back to the castle, having enjoyed their harmless masquerade as gentlemen. Felicity, like her sisters, was given a present of pin money by her mother every quarter day, and it was with that money that she had purchased disguises for both of them.

The advantage of the popularity of The Green Dolphin was that neither the landlord nor the serving maids had much time to wonder about the identity of the heavyset 'gentleman' and his 'nephew.'

Felicity threw the ostler a coin and told him to stable their horses, for the rain had started to fall. In fine weather, they left them tethered outside.

Miss Chubb entered the taproom first and

then drew back abruptly, bumping into Felicity who was behind her.

'What's the matter?' hissed Felicity.

'Come back outside,' muttered Miss Chubb.

But the landlord, Mr. Saxon, had recognized them as the two pleasant gentlemen who infrequently patronized his hostelry.

'Enter!' he cried. 'We have a deal of fine folk with us tonight. But I have your usual table at the window.'

'I don't know . . .' began Miss Chubb, but Felicity lowering her voice several registers, said heartily, 'Splendid, Saxon,' and, walking past Miss Chubb, she entered the tap.

A hum of voices rose to greet her. Apart from a few of the locals, there was a party of richly dressed men who had put two tables together in the middle of the room. Mr. Saxon guided Felicity over to the little table in the bay of one of the windows where she usually sat. With a feeling of apprehension, Miss Chubb lumbered after Felicity.

Usually, they had only the locals to contend with—locals who were interested in gossiping to one another and not bothering to pay too much attention to the two quiet gentlemen in the bay.

But these strangers were a different matter. When Mr. Saxon himself had served them with their usual glasses of claret, Miss Chubb whispered, 'We should not stay long, Felicity.

10

These strangers may become overcurious.'

Felicity was not listening to her. She was studying the men at a table in the center of the room with interest.

They were all dressed in riding clothes, and, from their conversation, she gathered they had all been guests at a shooting party at an estate farther along the coast. There were six of them. Their riding clothes were all well-cut as the finest morning dress and each man wore an expensive jewel in his stock.

But it was the man at the head of the table who held Felicity's attention the most. Once she had seen him, she found it almost impossible to look away.

He was quite old, she decided, about thirty years, and that *was* old in Felicity's eighteen-year-old eyes. He had a strong face with a proud nose and a firm chin. His eyes were very black and sparkling and held a clever, restless, mocking look. His brown riding coat was fitted across a pair of powerful shoulders, and his long legs encased in top boots were stretched out under the table. A ruby glittered wickedly in his stock and a large ruby ring burned on the middle finger of his right hand. His hands were very white and his nails beautifully manicured and polished to a high shine with a chamois buffer. Felicity was fascinated. Effeminate and decadent men were laughable; decadent and powerful men, such as this one, frightening.

'Do not stare so,' whispered Miss Chubb urgently.

But as if conscious of Felicity's curious gaze, the man looked across at her.

'Gentlemen!' he called. 'If you are so interested in our conversation, pray join us.'

A gentleman next to him, who had his back to Felicity and Miss Chubb, swung round and stared at them rudely through his quizzing glass.

'Never say they are gentlemen, Bessamy,' he drawled. 'Just look at the rustic cut of that lad's coat.' The other four solemnly produced their quizzing glasses and raked Felicity and Miss Chubb up and down as if studying two new and curious insects.

Then, as if finding them lacking in any merit whatsoever, they dropped their glasses and continued to talk about sport.

Miss Chubb let out a slow breath of relief. Felicity's face flamed.

'Pay no attention, my dear uncle,' she said in a clear, carrying voice. ' 'Tis naught but some city mushrooms aping the rudeness and the churlishness of the Corinthian set.'

There was a shocked silence. Miss Chubb muttered prayers under her breath. One of the gentlemen, the one next to the man called Bessamy, rose to his feet and slowly picked up his gloves.

'He's going to challenge you to a duel,' squeaked Miss Chubb.

Then Bessamy rose to his feet and with one hand pushed his friend down into his chair.

'Do not squabble with the locals,' he said calmly. 'Too fatiguing for words, and I have been bored enough this evening. Down, James, down, boy.' He picked up his glass and, to Miss Chubb's horror, crossed over to their table, pulled up a chair, and sat down.

Felicity turned her head away.

'Permit me to introduce myself,' he said. 'Bessamy. Lord Arthur Bessamy, at your service.'

'Charmed,' said Miss Chubb gruffly.

'And you are . . . ?' pursued Lord Arthur, his wicked black eyes fastened on Felicity's face.

Miss Chubb pulled her wide-awake hat down firmly over her eyes. 'I am Mr. George Champion,' she said, 'and this, my lord, is my nephew, Mr. Freddy Channing.'

Lord Bessamy swung his gold quizzing glass on its long, gold chain slowly back and forth, still looking at Felicity. Miss Chubb watched the pendulum swing of that quizzing glass with large, hypnotized eyes.

'And have *you* nothing to say for yourself, young fellow-me-lad?' asked Lord Arthur gently. 'You have just sorely insulted my guests and me. An apology would not come amiss. Or do you like dueling so much?'

Felicity forced herself to look at him. 'Your friends were very rude,' she said. 'But I admit I was rude, too, and for that I apologize.'

13

'Gracefully said, Mr . . . er . . . Channing. Hey, landlord, another bottle here.'

'We must leave, my lord,' said Felicity, trying to rise to her feet, but he pushed her back into her chair in the same autocratic manner as he had dealt with his offended friend.

'No, you must join me in a glass of wine. I insist.'

Miss Chubb groaned inwardly. In these days of hard drinking, she and Felicity were very abstemious, both of them preferring the taste of lemonade to wine. They only drank wine as part of their adventure, part of their masquerade. Both had admitted in the past that two glasses were definitely their limit. They had once experimented with a third but had found themselves becoming dangerously tipsy and inclined to relapse into their normal, feminine voices, instead of maintaining their adopted masculine ones.

Miss Chubb watched miserably as the bottle of wine was brought to the table. She knew she must rescue Felicity. There must be some way she could create a diversion. She rose to her feet.

'By your leave, my lord,' she said. 'I beg to be excused.'

'But we have not broached the bottle,' said Lord Arthur.

'I shall return very shortly.'

'But where do you go?'

'To the Jericho,' replied Miss Chubb, an ugly flush mounting to her cheeks.

'My dear sir, it is raining like mad. There are plenty of chamberpots in the sideboard over there, and we are all men here. I suggest you avail yourself of one.'

'But the serving maids . . .' put in Felicity quickly.

'Are not in the room at present,' he pointed out amicably.

'I insist on going outside,' barked Miss Chubb truculently.

She hurried off. Lord Arthur watched her departure with raised brows and then turned to Felicity.

'Do you belong to these parts, Mr. Channing?'

'Yes, my lord.'

'Channing . . . let me see. Ah, I have it. I have heard of a Mr. Channing of Tregarthan Castle.'

'Not him, nothing to do with him. Anyway, he's dead.' Felicity took a great gulp of wine to cover her confusion.

'How odd to have two Channing families in the same neighborhood and yet not related. This room is warm. Do you not wish to remove your hat?'

But Felicity knew if she removed her curly-brimmed beaver it would reveal her long hair piled up on top of her head. It was the custom for gentlemen to keep their hats on if they only

15

meant to stay somewhere for a short time.

'I must leave soon,' she said. 'I have pressing business.'

'That being . . .?' Felicity surveyed this handsome lord with great irritation. Why did he ask so many questions? Then a thought struck her. If he could be made to believe she belonged to the shop-keeping class, he would probably remove himself from her table and go back to his friends.

'I am in the tailoring business, my lord,' she said. 'Apprentice to a Mr. Weston.'

'But not the great Weston, as I can see from the cut of your coat. A tailor's lad, hey? Your master spoils you. I have never before seen a tailor's boy with such white hands.'

He filled her glass again.

'Tailoring is not hard labor,' pointed out Felicity. 'But now that you know I am well below your class, you will no doubt wish to remove to . . .'

'You do yourself an injustice, Mr. Channing. I find your company quite fascinating. What is it like being a tailor's apprentice?'

Felicity took a deep breath, another gulp of wine, and prepared to lie. Where on earth was Miss Chubb?

Miss Chubb had at first headed for the outside privy. The rain was falling hard. As soon as she was sure she was unobserved, she veered off in the direction of the stables. There had been no more arrivals since she and

16

Felicity had come to the inn, so the stable boys were in the tack room, sitting around the fire. She put her head round the tack room door and said she would lead out their horses and the boys were not to trouble disturbing themselves—something they were glad to agree to, none of them wanting to go out into the rain when they did not have to. Miss Chubb then took her horse and Felicity's and tethered them to a post in the yard of the inn over by the gate into the yard, but well away from the inn door.

Now, for that diversion.

Fear for Felicity sharpened her wits and made her brave. She returned to the stables and took a bale of hay and a small oil lamp. She carried the hay to the ground under the bay window at the side of the inn, behind which Felicity sat with Lord Arthur. The diamond-shaped panes of the windows were so old, so warped, and so small, she had no fear of anyone inside the inn being able to look out and see her.

She poured the oil from the lamp over the hay, took out her tinder box and tried to set it alight. The trouble with using a tinder box was that you had to be very lucky to get a light the first time. Often it took half an hour. Miss Chubb groaned. This looked like it would be one of the half-an-hour times.

Inside the inn, apparently enthralled, Lord Arthur Bessamy listened to Mr. Channing's

17

highly fanciful tale of life as a tailor's apprentice. Rather muzzy with wine, Felicity kept talking and talking, frightened that if she stopped, he might ask more questions. And so this Scheherazade of The Green Dolphin launched into a long and complicated story about a fat man who had insisted on trying on a coat made for a thinner gentleman, insisting it must be the one he had bespoke because it 'fitted him like a glove.'

She had just got to the interesting point when the tailor had challenged the fat man to a duel rather than let him take a coat made for another customer, when the room began to fill with black smoke.

Lord Arthur seemed unmoved. He kept his black eyes fastened on Felicity's expressive face. But his friends had jumped to their feet.

And then through the thick, rain-smeared glass of the windows came the red glow of fire.

Not knowing Miss Chubb was responsible for it, Felicity saw, all the same, a golden opportunity to escape from Lord Arthur.

'Fire!' she screamed. 'The stables are on fire.'

The tap room broke into an uproar, men fighting after Felicity to get out to rescue their precious horses.

Miss Chubb seized Felicity as she erupted out of the inn door.

'Straight to the gate,' she whispered urgently. 'The horses are there.'

With remarkable speed for such a heavy woman, Miss Chubb darted off with Felicity speeding behind her.

Lord Arthur's friends rushed straight to the stables. Only Lord Arthur, sauntering lazily to the front of the bay window at the side of the inn, found out where the flames were coming from. Or had come from. For the pounding rain was quickly reducing the once-flaming hay to a blackened mess.

He looked down at the hay, and then swung about as the clatter of hooves fleeing off into the night reached his ears. Then he returned to the inn.

Soon his baffled friends came back, exclaiming that they could not find the fire anywhere.

'Probably our imaginations,' drawled Lord Arthur. 'More wine, gentlemen?'

Felicity and Miss Chubb reined in their mounts at the top of the cliff. The governess told Felicity of how she had set the fire to cause a diversion. 'You are really very clever and bold, Miss Chubb,' said Felicity. 'I declare, I am proud of you.'

Miss Chubb blushed with pleasure in the darkness. 'I am glad I was able to be of help, Miss Felicity,' she said. 'Lord Arthur Bessamy is a most terrifying man.'

'Indeed, yes,' agreed Felicity with a shudder, thinking of those clever, searching black eyes. 'At least we need not trouble about him anymore and need not bother our heads about him again . . . thanks to you.'

But in her bed that night, as a fierce gale whipped round the castle and moaned in the arrow slits, Felicity lay awake, plagued by memories of Lord Arthur Bessamy. She had never met anyone like him before.

'And probably never will again,' said a gloomy voice in her head. 'Not the sort of gentleman to be pressed into marriage with anyone, and a cut above your stepfather's usual choice of husband.'

A large tear ran down her nose, and she brushed it away. She had drunk far too much and become maudlin, she told herself severely. Who in her right mind would want the terrifying Lord Arthur Bessamy as a husband? She pulled the pillows round about her ears to drown out the crying of the wind, and plunged down into an uneasy dream where she was sitting cross-legged on the floor of a tailor's shop stitching a wedding coat for Lord Arthur Bessamy, who was to be married the next day to the Queen.

*   *   *

Before he set out the following morning, Lord Arthur Bessamy made inquiries in the village for a tailor's assistant called Freddy Channing, but did not look in the least surprised to find no one had ever heard of the boy.

CHAPTER TWO

For the next two weeks, life at Tregarthan Castle returned to normal—that is, normal for Tregarthan Castle.

Mrs. Palfrey lay on a chaise longue in the drawing room during the day, sleeping or reading novels, or writing long letters to friends with whom she often corresponded, saying she was still too ill to receive visitors. The physician had diagnosed 'a wasting illness,' and had recommended quiet. In fact, Mrs. Palfrey would have been greatly cheered by a visit from some of her old friends, but Mr. Palfrey frowned on that idea, insisting that such excitement would be bad for her health, but privately thinking that his wife's friends were blessed with too many children—children who might chip the gloss on the legs of the furniture and make slides on the glassy surface of the floor.

Felicity stayed in the nursery wing with her governess, sharing all her meals with Miss Chubb as usual, rather than face formal dinners with her stepfather in the chilly, polished dining room where only a very small fire was allowed to battle with the winter cold, as a large fire might create more dust and ash to sully the pristine surfaces of tables and glass cases.

Although she should have been glad that no sign of an arranged marriage had reared its ugly head, she was bored. Very bored. The brief meeting with Lord Arthur had shown her a glimpse of a heady world of sophistication, a world where ladies could expect to be allowed one Season in London and have at least a chance of finding someone suitable out of a selection of gentlemen. But Mr. Palfrey would never countenance the expense of a Season.

The rain had fallen steadily since her visit to The Green Dolphin with Miss Chubb. Both ladies had been confined to the castle. But at the end of the second week since their 'great adventure' as Miss Chubb called it, the wind shifted to the east and then died down. Frost glittered on the lawns on the other side of the frozen moat and icicles hung down in front of the nursery windows.

Felicity and Miss Chubb were just getting warmly dressed, preparatory to going for a walk, when a liveried footman appeared with a message from Mr. Palfrey. Miss Felicity was to present herself in the drawing room immediately.

'Marriage!' whispered Miss Chubb as soon as the footman had left.

'I do not think so,' said Felicity. 'No one has come to call.' She giggled. 'They might leave wet footprints on Mr. Palfrey's precious floors. I shall not be long. Meet me in the hall.'

Mr. Palfrey was seated in a wing chair in front of the small fire in the drawing room. Lying on the chaise longue drawn up in front of the window was Mrs. Palfrey, her eyes closed, a piece of half-finished embroidery lying on her lap.

'Come in, Felicity,' said Mr. Palfrey, 'and sit opposite me. I have good news for you.'

Felicity sat down in a tapestried chair opposite. The pair surveyed each other cautiously.

Mr. Palfrey decided again that Felicity could hardly be classed as a beauty. There was something so . . . *wayward* about her appearance, and always a hint of rebellion at the back of those wide, innocent eyes.

Felicity was always struck afresh each time she saw him by how petty, nasty, and ridiculous her stepfather looked.

His sparse, graying hair was teased and combed back on top of his head. His blue morning coat was padded on the shoulders, and his cravat was built up high to cover the lower part of his face. He had a long thin body and very short legs, legs that were encased in skintight, canary-yellow pantaloons. With his thin yellow legs and his crest of hair, he looked like Mr. Canary in a children's story book. He had a little beak of a nose and very pale blue eyes.

'What news, Mr. Palfrey?' asked Felicity. After his marriage to their mother, Mr. Palfrey had begged the little Channing girls to call him 'Papa.' But not even the biddable elder girls had been able to call him that. He was so fussy, prissy, and spiteful that not one of them could view him in the light of father, so all had continued to call him Mr. Palfrey.

The castle was very quiet. The servants were expected to remain unseen and unheard as they went about their duties. If Mr. Palfrey came across, say, a housemaid, who had not time to run and hide, she was expected to turn her face to the wall and try to look as invisible as possible until he had passed.

The clock on the mantelpiece ticked a rapid chattering tick-tack, and a flame spurted out of a log in the fire and died, while Mr. Palfrey considered his reply.

'I credit you with a natural modesty and humility, Felicity,' said Mr. Palfrey. 'So it may have occurred to you that you are not *exactly* pretty.'

'Not in a fashionable way, no,' said Felicity mildly.

'Not in *any way at all*,' said Mr. Palfrey sharply. 'I have therefore had some difficulty in finding you a suitable husband.'

Felicity went very still and tense. Who? Who? Who have you found for me? chattered an anxious voice in her brain along with the restless chatter of the clock.

Mr. Palfrey made a steeple of his fingers and looked at Felicity over them. 'There is, moreover, a shortage of young men. You cannot expect a *young* husband such as your more fortunate sisters have found.'

'Maria married the Bishop of Exeter,' said Felicity tartly, 'and he is in his forties.'

'Enough!' said Mr. Palfrey, holding up one hand. 'But you will consider yourself fortunate when you hear that I have found a suitable gentleman for you. A titled gentleman.'

'Who is?'

'Lord St. Dawdy.'

A faint moan came from the direction of the window. Felicity looked anxiously at her mother, but that lady still lay with her eyes closed, apparently asleep.

'You are not going to marry me off to anyone,' said Felicity in an urgent whisper, her eyes blazing, 'least of all to an ancient gentleman who has been married twice before. Besides, he is abroad.'

'You have no choice in the matter,' said Mr. Palfrey. 'The baron has returned and has honored me by accepting my proposal. You will marry him or be thrown out of here.'

'You cannot throw me out of my own home! Mama would never allow it. You would be the laughingstock of the neighborhood.'

'I weary of trying to cultivate the goodwill of the peasantry. They may think me hard-hearted, if they wish. Once you are safely married, they will come about.'

Felicity looked at him, appalled. She had

25

never really dreamed he would go this far.

'Let me tell you this, Mr. Palfrey,' she said, leaning forward, her eyes flashing, 'you have not yet taken my measure. I am not meek and quiet like my sisters. I shall not let you force me into marriage. *I shall not let you!'*

Her voice had risen. Mrs. Palfrey stirred and moaned again.

'Don't, Felicity,' she said weakly.

Felicity ran to the window and knelt down by her mother and took one of Mrs. Palfrey's thin, wasted hands in her own. 'Mama,' she said, 'he says I am to marry Lord St. Dawdy.'

Mrs. Palfrey's eyes glittered with tears. 'Mr. Palfrey,' she started to say, 'I do beg of you . . .' but the rest of what she had been going to say was lost in a bout of asthmatic wheezing.

'Now look what you have done!' exclaimed Mr. Palfrey, fussing forward. 'Leave us immediately.'

Felicity rose and stood looking mutinously at her stepfather, prepared to do battle. But her mother's weak plea of 'Yes, my dear, do leave us' went straight to her heart.

'I am going for a walk on the grounds with Miss Chubb,' said Felicity, 'and when I return, Mr. Palfrey, and when Mama is not present, we shall discuss this matter further.'

She turned and ran from the room.

When she had gone, Mrs. Palfrey tried to struggle up. 'Do not do this to Felicity,' she gasped. 'You misjudge her. She has strength and spirit, very like her father.'

'That spirit is unbecoming in a young miss,' said Mr. Palfrey, extracting a Limoges snuffbox and taking a delicate pinch. 'St. Dawdy will soon break her to harness. Now, do not distress yourself over the tiresome child. I am going to ride over to St. Dawdy's to discuss the marriage settlement.'

After he had left, Mrs. Palfrey fumbled in her sleeve for her handkerchief and dried the tears that had begun to flow over her white cheeks. Then she rang a bell placed on a little table beside her.

'Giles,' she said to the footman who answered it. 'Has Mr. Palfrey left?'

'Yes, ma'am, just this second. Shall I call him back?'

'No, no. I want you to go out on the grounds or even beyond, to find Miss Felicity, who is out walking with Miss Chubb. Bring her back to my bedchamber. Send Benson to help me upstairs.' Benson was the lady's maid.

Meanwhile, Felicity and Miss Chubb had retreated to the one uncultivated corner of the garden by the south wall where a curtain of creeper drooped over a tangled mass of wildflowers, their winter leaves yellow and brown—mallow, foxglove, borage, and rosebay willow-herb. The rest of the garden about the castle was as manicured and ordered as the inside of the great building. Grass, cut into geometric patterns, surrounded the rosebeds;

27

the roses were never allowed to grow to any height but were always ruthlessly pruned so that only a few regimented flowers were allowed to bloom each summer.

This one corner had, so far, escaped Mr. Palfrey's notice, and Felicity found it a soothing place to go, a place mercifully free of his fussy, nagging perfectionism.

She had told Miss Chubb about the marriage that had been arranged for her, stoutly maintaining that she would not be forced into it, and Miss Chubb listened, her heavy face drooping and her doglike eyes sad, for she really did not think Felicity, as her stepfather had pointed out, had any choice in the matter at all.

Felicity looked up after her defiant statement of independence and saw the footman, Giles, hurrying toward her.

'He wants me back for a further argument,' she said gloomily. But as soon as she heard it was her mother who wished to see her, she ran like the wind. Felicity had not seen her mother alone for some time, Mr. Palfrey having forestalled any efforts in that direction.

It had been many years since Mrs. Palfrey had shared a bedchamber with her husband. But her own bedchamber had not escaped her husband's reorganizing zeal. The floor was slippery with beeswax and ornamented with an Oriental rug placed with geometric precision exactly in the center of the floor. Her bed was of the newfangled kind that Felicity detested, having neither posts nor curtains, but shell-shaped and draped with a cover of chilly white lace.

'Come in, my dear,' said Mrs. Palfrey faintly. 'I do not have much time.'

Mrs. Palfrey was now sure she was dying, but Felicity thought her mother meant that she had not much time before her husband came back.

'Now, don't interrupt me,' said Mrs. Palfrey feebly. 'Sit down on the end of the bed and listen. I have not been a good mother. No! You must not interrupt. I allowed Mr. Palfrey to arrange marriages for my other girls. It seemed as if he had good sense, for Penelope and Emily appear to be content, and I can only pray that Maria will find the same happiness. But from what I have heard of the baron, he is not the man for you, or indeed for any woman. You must have your independence, Felicity. Mr. Palfrey does not, I believe, know of the Channing jewels. I did not tell him about them. I knew he loved beautiful things, and I had planned to dazzle him with a display of them after we were married. I did not then know how greedy he was—but I soon found out.

'Before I fell ill, I hid the box with the jewels. It may surprise you to know there is a priest's hole in this castle.'

'But I do know,' said Felicity, wondering. 'I

29

have been in it.'

'There is a ledge up at the top of it. You probably never looked up there. It is hard to see in the blackness. You will find an iron box there. That is your dowry. I shall leave them to you in my will, and you must point out to Mr. Palfrey that with such an enormous dowry, you may marry whom you please. In the meantime, appear as if you have decided to accept the baron. I do not wish to die without having made some provision for you.'

'Mama! You will live a long time. Perhaps another physician should be called.'

'Perhaps I shall live longer than I expect,' said Mrs. Palfrey with a weak smile, 'but we shall try for a stay of execution. I shall tell Mr. Palfrey I do not wish you to be married until I am well enough to attend the ceremony. The Channing money is still mine, and at least I have that hold over him, though I have never used it before.

'Now, I wish to add a codicil to my will, leaving you the jewels. I need two servants to be witnesses, but I must have two who are trustworthy and who will not talk to Mr. Palfrey or to anyone else.'

'There is John Tremayne, the head groom,' said Felicity slowly, 'and he will know of another who is as loyal to the Channings.'

'Fetch him quickly. Now.'

'But, Mama. You are making me afraid with this talk of death.'

'I have no time at the moment to talk to you further, my child. Go!'

Felicity longed to take her mother into her arms, to try to beg her to leave the castle and perhaps go to London where a physician might be better qualified to diagnose her illness. But fright and agitation were making Mrs. Palfrey's breath come in ragged gasps. Felicity left to go in search of John Tremayne.

After a short time, John Tremayne appeared with a housemaid, Bessie Redhill. The head groom was half in love with Bessie, who was plump and motherly.

Mrs. Palfrey asked Bessie to help her over to her writing desk. She pulled forward a sheet of parchment and then hesitated. She was suddenly consumed with hatred for this husband of hers who had only pretended to love her and whose greed and spiteful bullying character had become evident right after the wedding. Up until this moment, she had kept such feelings at bay, thinking them sinful. She had sworn in church before God to love and obey her husband, and she had tried so very hard to abide by the premise. But the fear that time was running out for her sparked the first strong feeling of rebellion Mrs. Palfrey had ever had. Why not leave everything she possessed to Felicity? It would only mean writing a very short will. Felicity could be trusted to share the money with her sisters and look after any servants who might have to be pensioned off.

She began to write quickly, while John and Bessie stood by, trying to mask their curiosity. At last she was finished, and she asked them both to sign. John Tremayne was illiterate and made his mark. Bessie had been educated at a dame school, and her bold, quick eyes traveled rapidly down the page before she signed.

Then she helped Mrs. Palfrey back to bed and left the room with John Tremayne.

When the servants had reached the stair landing, John asked, 'What was that all about, Bessie? Was it her will?'

Bessie hesitated. It was a great secret, that will; a rare secret. She decided to hug the knowledge to herself. The housekeeper, Mrs. Jessop, was always sneering at her. It would be nice after Madam died to startle the servants hall by saying that she, Bessie, had been witness to the will that was driving Mr. Palfrey mad with rage.

'Dunno,' she said laconically. 'Warn't time. I just signed my name without reading it.'

'Well, I hope there's something in there for Miss Felicity,' said John. 'Give us a kiss, Bessie. No one's around.'

Bessie giggled and kissed him on the lips, privately thinking that John Tremayne was a bit of an old goat. Then the servants went downstairs together.

*　　　*　　　*

At the time the servants were signing the new will, Lord Arthur Bessamy was strolling into his club, Boodle's, in St. James's. Boodle's was not a club for the politically-minded, like White's, which favored the Tories, or Brooks's, which had a membership of Whigs. It was a more comfortable place with the convenience of a 'dirty room' in which members, who had failed to dress for dinner were segregated.

Lord Arthur made his way to the coffee room, and there, sitting by the fireplace under the Abraham Hondius painting, *Stag Hunt*, he recognized the wilting figure of his friend, Charles Godolphin.

'You look,' said Lord Arthur pleasantly, 'about the sickest thing in London, Dolph. There is an inn in Cornwall called The Green Dolphin that would suit your complexion perfectly.'

'Been drinking Blue Ruin,' groaned Mr. Godolphin. 'Don't tower over me, there's a good chap. Sit down, do. Craning up at you makes my head ache.'

Lord Arthur sat down and surveyed his friend. Dolph was a tubby man, so small that his plump legs, encased in black Inexpressibles, did not reach the floor. His starched cravat supported two chins, and his short-sighted green eyes were crisscrossed that day with little red veins. He had teased his thick head of fair hair into the Windswept that morning, only to see it spring back into its normal style which resembled the thatched roof of a Tudor cottage. In despair, he had told his man to set it by using a mixture of sugar and water. That had seemed to do the trick, although it had given his hair a rigid, stand-up appearance that made him look as if he had been struck by lightning. The sugar and water mixture had dried on the road to the club, and the little crystals of sugar now decorated the shoulders of his coat like some exotic type of dandruff. A pair of new corsets was playing merry hell with his swollen liver. In all, Dolph felt terrible.

'Did you mention The Green Dolphin?' he asked, as Lord Arthur sat down in a chair opposite him.

Lord Arthur nodded. 'I was thinking of an inn of that name down in Cornwall, near Tregarthan Castle.'

'I know it,' said Dolph. 'Deuced good food. I had to escape there from the claws of a grasping relative.'

'Which one?'

'My Uncle Frank. He's Lord St. Dawdy. You know I'm always short of the ready, and I've been dipping deep. It occurred to me that the old boy might look at me in a kindly way in his declining years. He jaunters to the Continent a lot—had just got back when I arrived on his doorstep. We had an abominable supper, everything put in a pie, Cornish-style, but with great heaps of pastry to make up for the absence of meat.

'Still, I thought my digestion might be able to stand it—just. I asked tenderly after his health and said he must be curst lonely. Lives in a drafty, miserable place which looks as if it had been built by gnomes on an off-day—you know, low, low roofs, beams that bang even such a small chap as myself on the head, and sloping floors. He grinned and winked at me—he's a gross, vulgar, brutish man—and said he would not be alone for very much longer. "Why not?" I asked, hoping he meant that he would soon be among heavenly company. He said he was getting married to a fine, lusty girl who would bear him sons. Well, after a rocket like that, there didn't seem much point in staying. I murmured something about urgent business and fled to the nearest hostelry—The Green Dolphin.'

Lord Arthur took out a lace-edged cambric handkerchief and flicked a piece of dust from one glossy hessian boot. 'When you were at The Green Dolphin,' he said, 'did you by any chance notice a weird couple of fellows in the tap—a big, heavyset man and a slim, pretty youth?'

'No one like that.'

'And what is the name of the lady your uncle is going to inflict himself on?'

'Felicity Channing.'

'Ah, that name again,' murmured Lord

35

Arthur. 'Is this Felicity indeed a girl—or only a girl to someone of your uncle's age?'

'You may be sure I asked, hoping the marriage would not come to anything, you know. But it seems that even if Miss Channing does not want the baron, she will be forced to marry him nonetheless.'

'I have heard of a Bartholomew Channing of Tregarthan Castle, although that was when I was in short coats. My father said he was an admirable gentleman.'

'Ah, but he died, and the widow married a Mr. Palfrey, a man-milliner sort of fellow, much despised by the locals. He arranged marriages for the elder three of the widow's daughters—not bad marriages as it turned out, but he has settled on my uncle for the youngest, and what he says goes.'

'How very gothic. Do you attend the wedding?'

'Have to. He may yet leave me something.'

Lord Arthur sighed and stretched. 'Take me along with you, Dolph,' he said finally. 'I have a whim to see that part of England again.'

*   *   *

Mr. Palfrey sat back in the carriage that was bearing him back to Tregarthan Castle and beamed with satisfaction. He had forced the baron to agree to only a very small dowry, explaining that Felicity's youth and beauty were dowry enough. He had had miniatures of all the girls painted as they reached the age of seventeen, but instead of showing the baron Felicity's miniature—for Mr. Palfrey privately thought Felicity a very poor sort of female in the looks department—he had shown him instead a miniature of Maria; Maria who had all the formal beauty of the Channings.

That had settled the matter, and the baron had almost drooled over that miniature and had agreed to the tiny dowry. Then Mr. Palfrey frowned. He did hope his wife was not going to make trouble over this marriage. But she had never made any trouble before. Still, she obviously doted on the odd little Felicity. Better to have a stern word with her.

But Mrs. Palfrey was beyond listening to any stern words. When he arrived in her bedchamber, it was to find her lying serene and tranquil in the endless sleep of death.

Before summoning the servants, Mr. Palfrey sat down at her desk so that he could prepare himself to act the part of grief-stricken husband. It was all his now, he thought in a sort of wonder. Tregarthan Castle, the Channing fortune, and the Channing estates. All his. It was tiresome that Felicity's marriage would have to be delayed while a decent period of mourning was observed.

He half rose from the desk. And then he saw his wife's Last Will and Testament. He lit more candles and sat down to read it with a fast-beating heart.

The spasm of fury that consumed him was so intense that he thought his heart would burst through his chest. He looked at Bessie Redhill's signature and then at John Tremayne's mark. The head groom was illiterate, and perhaps the maid had not read what she was signing. And what was this about the Channing jewels? What jewels?

The earlier will, leaving everything to him, reposed downstairs in his desk in the library.

He must burn this one, and then see if he could quiet those servants. He picked up the will and carried it over to the fire. But the fire had burned very low. He threw on some coal and eagerly waited for it to burst into a blaze.

The door opened and Benson, the lady's maid, walked in.

Mr. Palfrey thrust the will into the pocket in his coattails.

Benson was staring in anguish at the still figure on the bed.

'My beloved wife is dead,' said Mr. Palfrey. He thought again of that will, and tears of rage spurted out of his eyes. Benson said afterward she had never until that moment realized how very much Mr. Palfrey had loved his wife.

CHAPTER THREE

Felicity's courage appeared to vanish with the death of her mother. She was crushed down under a load of grief.

Her stepfather cried a great deal as well, but Felicity had noticed the strong smell of onion coming from his handkerchiefs and knew he was acting, but she did not even have the strength to become angry.

There was some comfort for her in the arrival of her sisters for the funeral. She was able to share her mourning and found a great deal of solace in noticing that not only Penelope and Emily appeared happy with their husbands, but that Maria was content with her bishop. He was a large man with a hectoring manner and a booming voice, but Maria appeared to hang on his every word. There was something to be said for arranged marriages after all, thought Felicity. Marriage to Lord St. Dawdy would at least mean having a home of her own.

Despite her grief, she could not help hoping the baron might ride over to attend the funeral, but Mr. Palfrey said Lord St. Dawdy detested funerals, and Felicity thought the baron must be a very odd man indeed to stay away from his intended bride's family mourning.

All too soon, Mr. Palfrey managed to fuss the sisters and their husbands out of the castle, which settled back into its usual deadly glacial quiet.

Felicity and Miss Chubb decided to go out riding the day after the Channing sisters had left, although the sky was darkening and there was a metallic smell of snow on the wind.

John Tremayne saw to the saddling of their horses himself. After he had helped Felicity up, he stood with his hand on her stirrup and looked up anxiously into her face.

'I do not wish to distress you, Miss Felicity,' he said, 'but has the will been read?'

'Yes,' said Felicity curtly, putting a hand down to pat her little mare's neck, for the animal had sensed her sudden rush of anger and had begun to fidget. 'It is as I expected. Everything goes to Mr. Palfrey.'

'But, miss, you remember when you came for me the day Mrs. Palfrey died? You told me to find another loyal servant because Madam wanted two witnesses? I took the maid, Bessie Redhill, with me. Madam gave us a piece of paper with writing on it to sign. I can't read nor write and though Bessie can, she said she didn't have time to see what was on the paper.'

'So, Mama did write that codicil,' said Felicity slowly.

'What . . . what was it, that thing you just said?'

'Look, John. I shall tell you and Miss

Chubb, but you must keep it to yourselves and not ever tell anyone, not even Bessie. Tell her only that the piece of paper was nothing important. You see, I believe my stepfather found that codicil which left Mama's jewels to me, and burned it. But I know where they are hidden, and I am not going to tell him!'

'I promise, miss. I'll never tell a soul, and if Bessie mentions that piece of paper, I'll deny it, that I will. It'll be her word against mine, and I think master'll be more inclined to believe an old servant.'

At that moment, a groom came running up and said John was wanted in the castle by Mr. Palfrey.

'He probably wants to ask you where I am,' said Felicity. 'Stand clear, John. Come along, Miss Chubb. Off we go!'

John made his way slowly toward the castle.

Bessie, who had also been summoned, arrived outside the library before him. She had hugged the knowledge of that other will to herself. Surely Mr. Palfrey would pay, and pay well, to have it kept a secret.

Mr. Palfrey had an extensive wardrobe. He had changed into the coat he had been wearing on the day of his wife's death. It was the first time he had worn it since then. He was sitting down at his desk in the library when he heard the crackle of parchment from the pocket in his tails. He drew out his wife's last will, cursing that he had not destroyed it before this. When he found the coat that morning, it had been folded in a chest with some papers in his bedchamber, and he had forgotten why he had thrust it there. It was as well he had not put the coat with his others, or his valet would have found the will when he cleaned out the pockets. Why on earth had he been convinced he had already destroyed the will? He had drunk long and deep on the night of his wife's death. His memory of thrusting that plaguey will between the bars of the library fire must have been a drunken dream. It must be got rid of at once! He bent over the library fire.

Then he heard Bessie's heavy footsteps approaching across the hall and crammed the will back into his pocket.

He eyed Bessie carefully as she walked in. She seemed a pleasant, motherly woman. Probably there would be no difficulty in dealing with her.

'I am afraid I must give you your notice, Bessie,' said Mr. Palfrey. 'With the ladies married and my poor wife in her grave, there is no longer any need to maintain such a large staff.'

'You're getting rid o' me because I know the missus wrote a last will leaving everything to Miss Felicity.'

'Nonsense!' said Mr. Palfrey, turning a muddy color.

The door opened, and John Tremayne

walked in.

Bessie looked at John triumphantly. 'I was just telling Master that we signed a will that Mrs. Palfrey wrote—the day she died, it was.'

John looked at her stolidly. 'I never signed anything,' he said.

'That you didn't,' said Bessie scornfully, 'you not being able to write, But you made your mark!'

Had Bessie told him that the will was one leaving everything to Felicity, John would have changed his tune. But he thought it was only that bit about the jewels he had witnessed, and Mr. Palfrey must never know about the jewels.

'I neither made my mark nor know anything about any will,' said John firmly.

Color began to tinge Mr. Palfrey's cheeks. He had been about to fire John as well, never having liked the relic of the Channing dynasty who had come to the castle as a little stable boy when old Mr. Channing was still alive, but the fellow was obviously beautifully stupid, and just what he, Mr. Palfrey, needed.

'There you are,' said Mr. Palfrey pompously, beginning to stride up and down. 'You may pack your things and leave this day Bessie.'

Bessie looked from one to the other, appalled. Without John to back her, she had no proof there ever was a will.

John started. 'I did not know you were getting rid of Bessie, Master,' he said. 'She is a

43

good maid, and 'tis hard to find work hereabouts.'

'That is not my concern,' said Mr. Palfrey, fortifying himself with a pinch of snuff.

John hesitated, almost tempted to tell the truth, because the dismissal of Bessie had shocked him. But two things, apart from loyalty to Felicity, made him stay quiet.

The first was that he had overheard Bessie joking with one of the other maids only a week before. The maid had been teasing, Bessie, saying John Tremayne was sweet on her, and Bessie had tossed her head and replied that she could do better for herself and had done nothing to encourage the attention of an old and smelly groom like John Tremayne. John, a wiry man in his forties with a pleasant, weatherbeaten Celtic face, had been badly hurt by the insult.

Added to that, he now surprised a look of cunning and greed in Bessie's eyes that changed her appearance entirely, making her look almost sinister.

He did not know that Bessie had seen the will poking out of Mr. Palfrey's back pocket as he strutted up and down the library. She now wanted to find some way to get her hands on it before Mr. Palfrey managed to destroy it.

'You'd best come with me, Bessie,' said John firmly. 'If Master says you have to leave, then leave you must.'

'Oh! Oh! *Oh!*' screamed Bessie, tearing her

cap off and throwing it on the floor. 'What will become of me? Please don't send me off.' She threw herself into Mr. Palfreys arms, nearly knocking him flat.

He tried to push her away, but Bessie clutched hold of him, and the ill-assorted couple did a macabre waltz over the polished floor.

With a great heave, Mr. Palfrey finally sent her flying. She stumbled backward and just managed to stop herself from falling.

But she had seized the will and had it hidden in the folds of her apron. Pretending to weep, she rushed from the room.

'You're a good man, John,' said Mr. Palfrey. 'You may go about your duties.'

'Why did you send for me?' asked John, curiously.

'Because . . . because I anticipated trouble with the maid and felt sure you would help to handle the situation. Where is Miss Felicity?'

'Out riding with Miss Chubb.'

'She should be accompanied by a groom. Now that she is soon to be a baroness, she must begin to observe the conventions. See to it.'

'Very good, sir,' said John, touching his forelock and bowing his way out.

Outside the library, he scratched his head. Mr. Palfrey would normally have instructed the housekeeper to get rid of Bessie. He must be worried about those jewels. John gave a slow smile. Well, Miss Felicity had them safe. Mr. Palfrey would never get them. Pity about Bessie. She had seemed such a kind woman before. John shook his head dismally over the fickleness and cruelty of women and made his way back to the stables.

* * *

Felicity and Miss Chubb swung down from their mounts at the cliff's edge, some distance from the castle. They tethered their horses to a stunted tree and both looked down at the wrinkled gray sea far below them.

'I know he burned that bit about the jewels,' said Felicity fiercely. 'He is a liar and a thief But he shall not have them!'

'You told me they were hidden in the priest's hole. Are there a great many jewels?' asked Miss Chubb.

'In truth, I never bothered to look inside the box. I have been too grief-stricken. I only checked to be sure it was there, where Mama said it was. Oh, poor Mama.'

Felicity turned her head away and began to cry. Miss Chubb shuffled her large feet like an old horse. She could not share in Felicity's grief, for Miss Chubb had always considered Mrs. Palfrey to be a very poor mother indeed. 'If Felicity were my daughter,' Miss Chubb told herself, 'then sick as I was, I would have yet found the strength to rid myself of such a nasty

46

character as Mr. Palfrey.'

She waited until Felicity had recovered and then said gruffly, 'At least this period of mourning has put your marriage off. With any luck the baron might die before the year is out.'

'Do you know, Miss Chubb,' said Felicity, 'this Lord St. Dawdy, though old, might be quite a pleasant sort of man.'

'You said your mama did not think so,' pointed out Miss Chubb. 'And he is not liked in the county.'

'People can be hard, particularly on absentee landlords,' sighed Felicity. 'And the baron has traveled a great deal. Besides, mama did not seem to be a great judge of people or she would not have married Mr. Palfrey. My sisters are content in their marriages. The arrangements worked out well for them. Penelope told me it was exceedingly pleasant to be mistress of one's own establishment and to have children. And I could take you with me.'

Miss Chubb brightened, but then her face fell. 'I cannot see any man countenancing the presence of an elderly governess.'

'But if I were a baroness, surely I could elevate you to the rank of companion?'

'Perhaps,' said Miss Chubb gloomily. 'But I would not count on it.'

'Look, the snow is beginning to fall,' said Felicity with a shiver. 'Perhaps when the weather is better, we can don our disguises and ride down to The Green Dolphin for another adventure.'

'I was frightened last time,' said Miss Chubb. 'Lord Arthur was a very unsettling sort of man.'

Felicity kicked a piece of turf. 'Do you think there are many men like Lord Arthur in London, Miss Chubb?'

'He was very handsome and very grand,' said Miss Chubb reflectively. 'No, not many.'

'It is of no use wondering about it,' said Felicity, 'for I shall probably never go to London. Or not as a single lady, anyway.'

They rode together back to the castle to hear John's story of the sacking of Bessie.

'Poor woman,' said Felicity. 'I have some pin money left. She may have it.'

When she and Miss Chubb entered the castle, the butler, Anderson, told them that Mr. Palfrey was searching everywhere for the blueprints to the castle and wondered if either of the ladies had seen them.

'No,' lied Felicity quickly. Mr. Palfrey must never find those blueprints, or he would discover the priest's hole.

She and Miss Chubb hurried up to the nursery, took the blueprints out of a desk, took them to the priest's hole, and put them up on the high ledge with the box of jewels.

Mr. Palfrey had just learned that one of his tenant farmers, Ebeneezer Pulkton, had called and was demanding audience. Mr. Palfrey hesitated, half-tempted to send the man away, for in his search for the blueprints he had not burned the will. Also, he wanted to study it again in peace so that he might be sure that bit about the Channing jewels—unaccountably absent from the previous will—was indeed there. But Mr. Pulkton was a toady, and Mr. Palfrey loved toadies—they being a rare commodity in Cornwall, where the population were singularly independent-minded and did not have a correct respect for their betters.

He had received a bad shock over that will. He longed to sit and drink a glass of port in congenial company. Mr. Palfrey had never felt lonely before. Now he did. In fact, he felt quite weak and helpless and wished his stern and domineering mother were still alive so that he could lay his weary pomaded head on her iron bosom.

'Show Mr. Pulkton in, Anderson,' he said, 'and bring us a couple of bottles of the best port.'

Mr. Pulkton entered, hat in hand, his little piggy eyes darting here and there as if seeking something that he could turn into a profit. He was dressed in a holland drill smock, breeches, and ankle boots. His smock had three capes on the shoulders, denoting his status as farmer. In this age of elegance, even the farmers were dandies, and the front of Mr. Pulkton's snowy-white smock was embroidered with scarlet

49

hearts.

'I din't like to come afore,' said Mr. Pulkton slowly. 'But I felt I must pay my respects, like. Terrible trajdy, Missus dying like that.'

'Yes, yes,' said Mr. Palfrey, giving his eyes a perfunctory dab with a wisp of handkerchief. 'Sit down, man, and join me in a glass of port. Ah, Anderson. The table by the window, and we shall serve ourselves.'

Mr. Pulkton looked suitably gratified.

*   *   *

As she sat on the edge of her bed in the room she shared with three other maids, Bessie heard the sound of approaching footsteps and thrust the will she had been studying under her mattress. She was alone, having been told to go and get her belongings, while the three more fortunate maids with whom she shared the room went about their duties.

Bessie started in surprise as Felicity walked in.

'I have heard of your dismissal, Bessie,' said Felicity awkwardly. 'Please take this money. It is not very much, but it will serve to keep you until you find another post.'

'Thank you, miss,' said Bessie. She had a sudden impulse to whip that will out from under the mattress and hand it to Felicity. Felicity had the same striking dark-red hair as her father, the same fascinating green-gold eyes. And Bessie remembered the late Mr. Channing very well. He used to throw open the castle once a year and entertain all the locals lavishly, a practice that Mr. Palfrey had not maintained.

But Miss Felicity was to marry a baron and would soon have all the money she wanted. Bessie knew that will could make her own fortune. She remained silent, and after giving the maid an embarrassed pat on the shoulder, Felicity left.

Bessie waited. She was to be allowed to stay the night before leaving in the morning. She must wait until she had guessed Mr. Palfrey had retired to his bedchamber and visit him there.

*   *   *

Mr. Palfrey climbed the stairs to his room after a euphoric drinking session with Mr. Pulkton.

His valet prepared him for bed, brushed out his sparse hair, gave him a glass of warm milk, and then left his master to sit by the fire.

Mr. Palfrey stared into the flames and sipped his milk. There was so much he could do now. He could fill the castle with the most beautiful treasures and become known around the world as a connoisseur of fine art. At last, he rose to his feet. Now for that will.

He was glad he had not burned it yet. There might be some hint, some clue, as to the whereabouts of the Channing jewels. He had told his valet to put his coat away without brushing it or emptying the pockets. He made his way to the wardrobe.

Behind him, the door opened.

Mr. Palfrey swung around.

Bessie Redhill stood there, smiling at him in a way he did not like at all.

'How dare you!' gasped Mr. Palfrey, one nervous manicured hand flying down to cover his private parts, although his nightgown was as thick as a bedsheet. With his other hand, he reached for the bellrope to summon help.

Bessie grinned broadly and held up the will.

With a squawk of outrage, Mr. Palfrey wrenched open the door of the wardrobe and scrabbled feverishly in the tail pockets of his coat.

Then he turned back to Bessie. His mind was working very quickly. The pleasant muzziness induced by his port-drinking session fled, leaving his brain sharp and clear.

He began to laugh. Bessie stared at him in surprise.

'You clever girl,' said Mr. Palfrey. 'So you've got the better of me after all!'

'Well,' said Bessie, closing the door and moving into the center of the room. 'I reckon we'll all be happy, sir, if we can do a deal.'

'Of course, of course,' said Mr. Palfrey, rubbing his hands. 'Sit down by the fire; there's a good girl.'

Bessie sat down gingerly, clutching the will.

'Now, a glass of brandy to warm us while we get down to business,' said Mr. Palfrey cheerfully.

'Don't mind if I do,' said Bessie with a broad smile. Mr. Palfrey looked so ridiculous with his little, spindly, hairy legs poking out from the bottom of his nightgown and with his red nightcap perched rakishly on the side of his head.

Mr. Palfrey went over to a cupboard in the corner and fiddled with bottles and glasses and came back with two bumpers of brandy.

He handed one to Bessie. 'Now, how much?' he asked pleasantly.

Bessie took a deep breath, her eyes glittering in the candlelight.

'Five hundred pounds.'

Mr. Palfrey stared. Five hundred pounds was a reasonable sum—very reasonable. But while he kept a smile on his face, his mind checked him by pointing out that Bessie would soon return for more. Like most of her class, she would probably drink to excess, drink would loosen her tongue, and before long the whole of the Duchy of Cornwall would know of his perfidy.

But just to make sure . . .

'And for five hundred pounds you will give me that will?'

'No,' said Bessie, an unlovely look of cunning crossing her plump features. She folded the single sheet of paper into a small square and thrust it into her bosom. 'Reckon I'll hang onto it for a bit.'

'As you will,' said Mr. Palfrey. 'A toast to seal our bargain. And to seal a bargain you must drain it to the last drop. Probably too much for you,' he said with a little laugh.

'Oh, I can take my drop,' grinned Bessie. She felt strong and powerful. She was now a lady of independent means. She would buy a silk dress and a carriage, and come calling on that housekeeper, Mrs. Jessop, and watch the old harridan's eyes pop out of her head.

She tilted the contents of her glass straight down her throat and then laughed and spluttered and gasped. Mr. Palfrey laughed as well and patted her on her plump shoulders.

'Now, wait here, Bessie,' he said, 'while I go to the strongbox and fetch you the money.'

He darted from the room, but only as far as the other side of the door. He waited, his heart thudding against his ribs until he heard the sound of a heavy body hitting the floor.

His thin lips curled in satisfaction.

He opened the door again and went in.

Bessie Redhill lay with her head on the fender, as still as death. He bent over her and pried open one eye. 'Still alive,' he muttered. 'Better move fast.'

He had tipped enough laudanum into her brandy to kill anyone of a less robust stature.

He dressed himself in his traveling clothes,

went downstairs, and roused his butler.

'Have my traveling carriage brought round to the front,' he said. 'I am going off on private business. I shall leave in about half an hour. I do not want any servant to be visible. Is that understood?'

Anderson bowed. He saw nothing odd in the request. Mr. Palfrey was always complaining about the servants. Unless actually serving him with something, he expected them to be invisible.

Mr. Palfrey went back upstairs, trying not to run. He took a large linen laundry sack out of a chest and with great difficulty, but with the strength of acute fear, managed to stuff Bessie's heavy body into it.

The carriage having been brought round, the servants kept well out of sight but listened in amazement to the crashes and bumps from the staircase.

Mr. Palfrey was not strong enough to lift Bessie on his back and so, piously thanking God for polished floors, he had slid his burden to the top of the stairs and proceeded to drag it down behind him.

Once outside, he almost gave up and called for help. He thought he would never be able to get Bessie inside the carriage. But at last, with one superhuman heave, he stuffed her inside and slammed the door.

He climbed up on the box and set off into the night. The snow had changed to sleet and drove into his face. But the madness of fear was on him, and he felt no discomfort.

He was grateful that the port of Falmouth was not many miles away.

In Falmouth, he went straight to a tavern he knew was frequented by sea captains and soon found the sort of character he wanted.

Captain Ferguson was only too pleased to have the 'present' of a fine, strong housemaid whom he could sell in America as a bonded servant. When Mr. Palfrey also gave him one hundred guineas, the captain swore lifelong friendship.

He saw nothing very odd or criminal in receiving a drugged body on board. In these days, when press-ganged victims could arrive bound and gagged, it was nothing much to take on the body of a drugged maid.

Luck was with Mr. Palfrey. The wind was fair, the good ship *Mary Bess,* would set sail before the morning, and when Bessie came out of her stupor—if she came out of her stupor, for he might have broken her neck dragging her down the stairs—she would be well on the way to the New World.

Anxious to remove himself from the vicinity as soon as possible, Mr. Palfrey did not stay at the comfortable inn, but set out on the road home, singing snatches of song as he bowled along the Cornish roads.

Once back, his long-suffering valet prepared his master for bed again. Mr. Palfrey kept having fits of the giggles, for all he had drunk, both with Mr. Pulkton and the sea captain, had finally gone to his head.

The bed seemed to have a tendency to run about the room. He glared up at the canopy, willing the room to stop spinning.

All at once he was stark, staring sober.

The will!

The will was still somewhere in Bessie's capacious cleavage.

His mind raced and spun as the drunken room had done only a few moments before.

And then he gave a deep sigh. What could a bonded servant do about anything? If she survived the journey, which was unlikely, she would be sold. She would not be paid a groat until her seven years of slavery were over. Surely no American was going to listen to a mere housemaid's babbling about some will. Salt water, or rats, or sweat, or any of the hazards of the journey would probably destroy that paper before Bessie ever reached America.

*   *   *

Felicity was crossing the hall the next day when she saw a woman dressed in black bombazine standing with her face to the wall.

'It is I, Miss Felicity,' she said impatiently.

'You may turn around, Mrs. Jessop.' Felicity thought Mr. Palfrey's treatment of the servants was disgraceful.

The housekeeper bobbed a curtsey. 'I heard the footsteps,' she said, 'and thought it was the master.'

'Has Bessie left yet?' asked Felicity.

'Yes, but it's ever so strange. She did not take a thing with her, and she even left fifteen pounds on her bed.'

'I gave her that money. I was sorry for her,' said Felicity.

'You shall have your money back, miss. Mr. Anderson has it in safekeeping. I would not feel sorry for Bessie. She could be lazy and a bit cruel with some of her remarks.'

'But if she left the money and her belongings, something may have happened to her,' cried Felicity.

'That's what I thought. But Mr. Palfrey told me he saw her slipping out of the castle last night, and he says as how one of his silver snuffboxes has been taken.'

'And did he inform the parish constable?'

'No, miss. He said he didn't want any scandal.'

'Thank you, Mrs. Jessop.' Felicity went up the stairs, wondering a little about Bessie's sudden turn to crime. Then her thoughts moved to her prospective marriage. She felt tired and beaten down, and weary with grief. She had not made any further protest about the marriage.

A little glowing image of Lord Arthur

Bessamy's handsome face rose before her eyes.

She gave a resigned shrug. Dashing and handsome and tantalizing men were for more fortunate females. Best put him completely out of her mind. She had not really liked him very much, so it was odd how much the memory of him kept returning to plague her. She would, in all probability, never see him again.

But Felicity was wrong.

CHAPTER FOUR

'Got a letter from that old rascal in Devon,' said Mr. Charles Godolphin to his friend Lord Arthur Bessamy.

Both men were strolling along the pebbly beach at Brighton, having followed the Prince Regent to that famous resort after the Season finished in June.

'Your uncle?'

'Yes, him. A most odd letter. He wants me to go there.'

'Has he decided to leave you his moneybags after all?' asked Lord Arthur.

'No, he's going ahead with this marriage. Wants to marry the girl in September.'

'Miss Felicity Channing is the lady, if I remember correctly. Is she proving difficult?'

'Well, this Felicity has, quite rightly I think, demanded a look at the goods first, or, to put it less vulgarly, she wants to see her intended.'

Lord Arthur looked amused. 'Do you mean they have never met?'

'Not even for a cup of tea. Whole thing was arranged by the girl's stepfather, Palfrey. The mother died last November and one would have thought they'd have waited until a year of mourning was over.'

'So why does Uncle Baron need Dolph?'

'He needs me because he says he's fallen madly in love with the chit.'

'A chit whom he has never set eyes on?'

'He's got her miniature,' said Dolph, 'and gazes at it night and day. He says he feels like a lovesick schoolboy.'

'Touching.'

'It would be,' said Dolph, stooping down, picking up a stone, and shying it out to sea. 'Only trouble is he's a satyr, a lecher, and a boor. Nevertheless, he wants me there to hold his paw and put in a good word for him with Miss Channing. I am to present myself at Dawdy Manor in two weeks' time.'

'My dear Dolph, if you intend to go, you had better set out now. It will take you all of that to get there—with your driving, that is.'

'Hoping you would drive me,' said Dolph.

Both men came to a stop. The sun was setting, and a sea gull called mournfully over their heads.

Lord Arthur gave a slight shrug. 'Why not, my friend? Why not? Nothing at all amusing has happened to me since I was last in Cornwall.'

*   *   *

Although it was quite cool within the thick walls of Tregarthan Castle, Mr. Palfrey was sweating profusely. He had just endured a terrible scene with his stepdaughter.

He had arranged a meeting for her with the baron, he had sent her measurements to London's finest dressmaker so that she might appear to advantage in the baron's eyes—and then he had commanded her to dye her hair brown, hoping to make her look as much like that miniature of Maria as possible.

And Felicity, who until that point had been meek, crushed, and biddable, with the one exception of demanding to meet her intended, had thrown back her head and let rip. She told him what she thought of him. She accused him of destroying her mother's health. The Holbein he had lately purchased would have repaired the tenants' cottages on the whole estate and have left plenty to spare, Felicity had raged.

The whole unsettling scene had brought all Mr. Palfrey's fears about Bessie rushing back. What if Bessie had shown that will to the captain or to anyone on board? The cunning captain would soon see the value of it. Why had he not killed her?

But Mr. Palfrey realized that, although he did not mind a rap if she died on board of cholera or typhoid, he could never bring himself to directly take away another's life.

And those jewels! He was weary with searching the castle from cellar to attic. There was a long portrait in the morning room of the late Mr. Channing's mother. She was in court dress and had a diamond tiara on her head and a fine diamond collar about her neck.

Where were the Channing jewels?

He was so upset, he decided he would have to brave the baron's possible fury. The marriage settlement had been signed. Surely the baron would not back out of the marriage just because Felicity had red hair and was not precisely handsome.

All his worries swirled about his head and settled down to focus on Felicity. With that redheaded jade out of the way, he could begin to lead an orderly and carefree life. He had not worried so much about Bessie for some time. It was Felicity's vulgar scene, which had rattled him so much, and brought all the fears rushing back.

Felicity, on the other hand, felt better than she had since her mother's death. That scene, that angry release, had brought all her confidence rushing back. She rode out with Miss Chubb, contemptuously dismissing the escort of a groom as 'one of Mr. Palfrey's more harebrained ideas.'

After they had gone a little way from the castle, Felicity slowed her pace to an easy amble and told Miss Chubb all about that splendid confrontation. 'I know red hair is not fashionable,' said Felicity, 'but to ask me to dye it!'

'He is very anxious for this marriage to take place,' said Miss Chubb.

'Pooh! It will not take place should I take this baron in dislike.'

'Have you thought,' said Miss Chubb cautiously, 'that should you decide not to marry the baron, and tell Mr. Palfrey about those jewels, he might simply claim them. He has every legal right.'

'John will swear to the codicil.'

'John Tremayne cannot read or write and has already sworn he did not sign anything. And Bessie has disappeared.'

Felicity frowned. Somehow, she had always regarded those jewels as an investment, as a dowry, as a trump card to slam down in front of her stepfather. How could she have been so naive?

Of course, she could take the jewels and run away. But what respectable jeweler was going to buy gems from a slip of a girl? And an unrespectable jeweler would belong to the criminal class and would no doubt pay her only a fraction of their worth.

'If I were a man!' she cried suddenly to the uncaring summer sky.

She thought of Lord Arthur Bessamy. He had probably never known what it was like to be pushed around in the whole of his pampered life. That was what gave him his great air of arrogance and command. That was why he chose friends of a lesser type of man, thought Felicity, her lip curling in contempt as she remembered the gentlemen who had stared at her through their quizzing glasses and had dismissed her as a bumpkin. Lord Arthur was no doubt as bad as Mr. Palfrey—only happy when in the company of toadies. She wished for a moment that she could see Lord Arthur again so that he might not go happily into his dotage without knowing how much she utterly detested him.

And yet . . . and yet, was he so very detestable?

He had kindly treated them to wine and had not turned a hair when she had said she was a tailor's apprentice. Damn Lord Arthur. Every time she thought of him, she became upset. Better to think of the baron.

Felicity, in her mind, had turned Lord Dawdy into a genial sort of fatherly man, a bluff, rough traveler who would no doubt be content to have her company during his declining years. Miss Chubb had, unwisely, done nothing to explode these dreams, thinking sadly that it was as well Felicity used her imagination to resign herself to her fate.

*   *   *

'Gad! Is this the place?' Lord Arthur slowed his team to a halt on a ridge and looked down in awe on Dawdy Manor.

It had started life as a single-storied Tudor dwelling. One hundred years later, a prosperous ancestor had tagged on a second story, much higher than the bottom one and with large windows ornamented with fussy stonework. It made the bottom of the building look as if it were slowly returning to the earth, an impression heightened by the vast quantity of ivy that clung to its walls.

'That's it,' said Dolph. 'Drive on, there's a good chap. I'm mortal sharp-set.'

Lord Arthur began to wish he had not come. He sensed bad cooking and worse drains waiting at the end of the road. It was folly to indulge a whim, to run off to Cornwall because a certain Freddie Channing and his peculiar uncle had sparked his curiosity and imbued the whole of the duchy with an air of novelty, which he now thought it probably did not possess.

'If your uncle is as clutch-fisted as you say he is,' said Lord Arthur, 'and keeps country hours, then you will not have any dinner until four in the afternoon, and it's now only twelve noon.'

It transpired that Lord Arthur was right. To Dolph's plaintive request for food, the baron replied sourly that they should have stopped for something to eat on the road. This business of luncheon was newfangled nonsense, and he would have nothing to do with it. But they would only have to wait a couple of hours to break their fast. Tea would be served at two o'clock when Miss Felicity arrived with her stepfather.

'It is as well I have arrived ahead of time,' said Dolph. 'Three days early, in fact.'

'Decided I didn't need your help,' said the baron. 'Anyway, you don't like me, and you're only here because you hope I'll leave you something in my will.'

'Yes,' agreed Dolph with what his friend, Lord Arthur, considered a singular lack of tact.

But the baron seemed not in the slightest put out. He fished in his pocket and pulled out a miniature. 'Here,' he said, 'cast your peepers on this beauty. That's my Felicity.'

'Very beautiful,' said Dolph. He glanced up at Lord Arthur to see his friend's reaction and was surprised by an odd sort of look of—could it be disappointment?—on that gentleman's face.

'Is it possible to have a tankard of something wet, baron?' asked Lord Arthur. 'The roads were dusty, and I've a devilish thirst.'

'There's water outside in the pump,' said Lord St. Dawdy ungraciously. 'My housekeeper will show you to your rooms, and I'll see you back here at two o'clock.'

While they waited for the housekeeper, Lord Arthur studied his host. He was a wreck of a man. One swollen leg, encased in bandages, was propped up on a footstool. He wore a grubby stock and an old-fashioned chintz coat covered with wine stains and snuff stains. He had a large round head covered in a Ramillies wig, a relic of his youth that had not been powdered or barbered for some time and had lost a great deal of its curl. Wisps of it fell about his bloated face, which was covered in angry red pustules.

The housekeeper, a thin, old, bent woman, dressed entirely in black except for an enormous starched cap, finally arrived and led them up a shallow flight of uneven stairs to their rooms.

Lord Arthur hoped the ceiling of his bedchamber would prove to be a little higher than those in the rest of the house, because he was tired of stooping, but it proved to be as low-ceilinged, sloping-floored, and dark as the rooms downstairs.

The air was stuffy and stale, and smelled of a mixture of bad drainage, damp, and woodsmoke. He walked over to the mullioned window and wrenched at the catch until he managed to open it. Warm, sweet air floated into the room on the slightest of summer breezes. He leaned his elbows on the sill and looked out.

The garden was a wilderness, but wild roses tangled and tumbled over everything in a riot of color. On a little rise to his left was a 'ruin,' one of those picturesque follies built in the last century when it was fashionable for the host to ask his guests, 'Would you care to promenade to my ruin?' It had originally housed a hermit, one of the locals whom the late baron had paid with a lifetime's free ale to sit in it and look wise and ancient. The hermit had died of a liver complaint and had never been replaced.

It seemed that the baron did not have menservants, for when Lord Arthur, finding no bell, shouted out into the corridor for washing water, an old chambermaid eventually appeared, bowed down under the weight of two brass-bound cans. Lord Arthur relieved her of her burden and asked for towels. She looked frightened and puzzled and then said she would try to find some.

'What on earth does the baron use when he washes?' demanded Lord Arthur, half-amused, half-exasperated.

'The master only washes at Michaelmas and Martinmas,' said the maid slowly.

'But when he washes his face?'

'Well, most times, me lord, he jist uses the bed hangings.'

She came back after about half an hour with

two paper-thin towels and a bar of kitchen soap. Lord Arthur cursed himself for not having brought his own valet. His Gustav, an energetic Swiss, would at least have bustled about and seen to his master's comfort.

He made a leisurely toilet, changing into a blue morning coat with plaited buttons, buff skin-tight trousers, and hessian boots. His deft fingers molded a snowy cravat into the Oriental, and he brushed his thick black hair until it shone with blue lights.

He heard the sound of horses' hooves in the distance and went back to the window and looked out.

At first he could see nothing but a moving cloud of white dust on the sunny road. Then he could make out an open carriage with two occupants driven by a coachman with a liveried footman on the backstrap. He heard Dolph clattering down the stairs, but he stayed where he was, watching the carriage as it turned in through the gates and began to bowl up the drive. The gentleman passenger appeared, as it drew closer, to be a fussily dressed man with a petulant face. The lady held a parasol, so he could not see her face.

The carriage rolled to a stop beneath his window. The footman hopped down from the back, went round, and opened the carriage door and let down a small flight of steps and assisted the lady to alight. She held up the skirts of her flounced muslin gown, exposing one delicate ankle to Lord Arthur's gaze.

She furled her parasol, then stood and looked about her.

Lord Arthur caught his breath. For this young lady was not the fashionable beauty of the baron's miniature. She was slim, dainty, and very young—definitely under twenty, he thought. She was wearing the very latest thing in 'transparent' hats—that is, a wide-brimmed frivolity of stiffened gauze through which her red hair gleamed like living fire.

With a feeling of excitement, Lord Arthur turned from the window and made his way downstairs.

*   *   *

'He is a bad landlord, this baron,' said Felicity, stabbing the dry earth with the point of her parasol. 'If he is as rich as you claim, why does he not put some money into his estates? He must be almost as clutch-fisted as you are yourself. But at least, Mr. Palfrey, it is only your tenants' houses you let go to rack and ruin. Lord St. Dawdy treats his tenants with equal unconcern, but also, unlike you, prefers to live in a slum.'

Mr. Palfrey turned pink with outrage.

'Guard your tongue, miss. Oh, if only you had dyed your hair.'

'My dear stepfather, is it not well over time that you told me why you wanted me to dye my

70

hair brown?'

Mr. Palfrey looked sulky. 'I sent the baron Maria's miniature.'

Felicity started to laugh. 'Choice,' she said. 'Very choice, Mr. Palfrey. You have indeed gone and shot yourself in the foot. Let us go in and get this charade over with. I am relieved I am not what the baron expects. For I would not be married to a miser.'

'You will behave, d'ye hear,' hissed Mr. Palfrey, 'or I will have you whipped.'

Felicity paled slightly before the venom in his eyes and face. Then with a toss of her head, she moved before him into the darkness of the house.

The old housekeeper held open the door of the drawing room. Felicity went inside. Two gentlemen rose to meet her. The third remained sitting.

Felicity recognized Lord Arthur immediately. Her eyes, a polite blank, her face guarded, she curtseyed and then looked hopefully at Dolph—for surely her fiancé could not be that disgusting old wreck by the table.

'My dear,' said Mr. Palfrey unctuously after Lord Arthur and Dolph had introduced themselves, 'here is the baron.'

'What's this?' cried Lord St. Dawdy, glaring awfully at Felicity. 'Who's this red-haired chit? Where's my beauty?' And he pulled out the miniature.

'You have been sent the wrong picture,' said Felicity, striving for calm. Why did Lord Arthur have to be here? She could easily have extracted herself from this painful situation quite calmly had he not been looking at her with those amused eyes. 'That is a portrait of my elder sister Maria, who married the Bishop of Exeter last year.'

'Oh, it is, is it?' raged the baron. 'Well, let me tell you, Palfrey, the wedding's off. You cheated me. You promised me a beauty, not . . . not this.'

Long afterward, Lord Arthur was to wonder why he had not remained silent. As it was, he said in glacial tones, 'My dear baron, your wits must be wandering. Miss Felicity has a very rare beauty—quite out of the common way.'

Mr. Palfrey brightened. All might yet be saved. 'Perhaps, my lord,' he said with a genteel cough, 'you might consider marrying my stepdaughter yourself. Her dowry is . . .'

'You vulgar little man,' said Lord Arthur in tones of contempt. 'Why don't you take her to Smithfield Market and put her on the block? How dare you treat any gently-bred miss in this common manner?'

'Now you mention it,' said the baron with a wicked gleam in his eyes, 'she's quite a filly. Walk up and down a bit.'

'I am not in the ring at Tattersall's,' said Felicity, gritting her teeth. 'No!'

'Suit yourself,' said the baron. 'Sit down. Sit

72

down. Here's tea.'

The little company arranged themselves round the table at which the baron was seated. It was not covered by a cloth, and because of the sloping floor it sloped as well so that guests and hosts were kept busy catching their teacups as they slithered to the edge of the table. The tea was weak and tasted dusty. The sandwiches looked as if they had been made some time ago, which indeed they had, the baron having entertained the vicar to tea two days before. He had ordered the housekeeper to keep the leftovers so that they might be served up again.

For once, Mr. Palfrey and his stepdaughter shared the same thought, but for different reasons—if only Lord Arthur Bessamy were not present!

Dolph began to chatter nervously about the Prince of Wales's recent appointment as Regent and of the splendid party he had given in Clarence House. The baron's brooding and lustful eyes fastened greedily on Felicity's rounded bosom.

Felicity began to feel faint. The room was close and warm, and the smell from the baron was something quite dreadful. Lord Arthur's exotic and unexpected presence upset her. If only he had kept quiet! Then the baron might have continued to be disappointed in her appearance.

But one thing sang in her head. She would

not marry the baron, no matter what happened. She had dreamed of an old and fatherly man, not this horrible, gross creature. She longed for Miss Chubb's reassuring company.

While Dolph rattled on, Mr. Palfrey and the baron exchanged looks and then the baron winked and nodded his head. Mr. Palfrey heaved a sigh of relief.

There was a smash as Dolph's teacup hit the floor. The rest were managing the peculiar exercise of leaving their cups for a moment, then catching them just as they slid to the edge of the table.

'You'll pay me for that,' said the baron. 'Why don't you take Miss Felicity outside for a walk, Dolph?'

Dolph jumped to his feet. Glad to escape, Felicity rose and accepted his escort. Lord Arthur followed them out.

They walked in silence through the sunny, tangled grounds, Felicity in the middle, Dolph on her left hand, Lord Arthur on her right. It was so bright, warm, and rose-scented that Felicity wondered bleakly why some of the sunshine could not light up the darkness in her soul.

'The weather is very fine, is it not?' ventured Dolph. Felicity lowered her parasol and withered him into silence with a look of contempt. Here she was, about to be forced into marriage with an old lecher, and this

London fool was babbling on about the weather.

'Tell me,' said Lord Arthur, 'have you ever met a tailor's boy called Freddy Channing?'

'No, my lord,' said Felicity loftily, as if such a person were definitely beneath her notice.

'Strange,' he murmured, 'in such a sparsely populated region, I felt sure you would know everyone hereabouts.'

'I do not go about much,' said Felicity repressively.

'Perhaps after your marriage ...'

'You are in error. I shall not marry, and certainly not Lord St. Dawdy.'

'But your stepfather seems very determined.'

'So am I,' said Felicity. 'What brings you here, Lord Arthur?'

'I came with my friend, Mr. Godolphin. He is Lord St. Dawdy's nephew.'

'And do you visit your uncle often, Mr. Godolphin?' asked Felicity.

'From time to time,' said Dolph, struggling with his stock, which appeared to have become very tight. He thought this ferocious little girl was proving to be an uncomfortable companion.

'You do not seem to be enjoying our company,' said Lord Arthur, a mocking note in his voice.

'No, I am enjoying none of this,' said Felicity. 'If you had not found it necessary to praise my appearance, Lord Arthur, then the baron might have cried off.'

'I am sorry, but then, I do find you beautiful, Miss Channing,' said Lord Arthur, a caressing note in his voice.

Felicity's face flamed, and she rounded on him. 'But you do not like me well enough to marry me,' she said evenly. 'Only to praise me in order to bait the baron.'

'I say,' bleated Dolph helplessly.

Lord Arthur looked down at Felicity with something approaching dislike. He had been toying with the idea of doing something in the way of knight-errantry. He had been considering proposing to Felicity himself, for she fascinated and intrigued him, and he was sorry for her.

But because of his wealth and his title, he was used to people toadying to him quite dreadfully. No one had dared to criticize him for years, except perhaps Dolph, but Dolph was a man. Men who were friends were allowed the occasional remark—but females, never!

'I should not for a moment consider marrying such a broad-spoken termagant as yourself,' he said, and then wondered why he immediately felt like a coxcomb. 'After all,' he went on quickly, 'I have no intention of marrying anyone. Dolph here will tell you I am a confirmed bachelor.'

'Then, since you have damned me as broad-

76

spoken,' said Felicity, smarting with hurt, 'I shall go further and tell you that I do not like you one little bit, Lord Arthur. You are making a bad day horrible by your sneering and indifferent presence. I wish . . . I wish you would go away.'

He looked down into her furious eyes and saw all the pain and fear there. His heart gave a lurch. 'Miss Felicity,' he began, but another aged and bent maidservant of the baron's materialized at his elbow to say that Mr. Palfrey was ready to leave and would Miss join him immediately.

Felicity ran off in the direction of the house.

'Phew!' said Dolph. 'I pity my uncle if he marries that shrew.'

'I behaved badly . . . very badly,' said Lord Arthur curtly. 'We are going to ride over to Tregarthan Castle tomorrow so that I may make my apologies.'

'But, I say . . .' said Dolph.

'There's going to be a storm,' said Lord Arthur, beginning to walk back toward the house. 'Clouds are piling up in the west.'

Dolph looked over to the west and saw a mountain of great, fat purplish clouds climbing up the sky. Then he hurried to keep up with his friend's long strides. Lord Arthur was behaving in a most odd way. Dolph began to wish he had not brought him.

*   *   *

Felicity and her stepfather each kept an icy silence on the road home. A great crashing peal of thunder rolled about the turrets of the castle as they entered the polished gloom of the hall.

Felicity was about to stalk off up the stairs, but Mr. Palfrey seized her arm in a vicious grip and started to call for his servants.

The butler, the footmen, the maids, and the housekeeper came hurrying into the hall.

Mr. Palfrey addressed them, still keeping tight hold of Felicity. 'My stepdaughter has disgraced me,' he cried. 'She is to be whipped!'

Felicity managed to pull free, and stood white-faced, looking at the servants.

Not one of them moved to obey the command. They stood stolidly, in a circle, looking at their master.

'Whip her!' screamed Mr. Palfrey, beside himself with rage.

Anderson, the butler, cleared his throat. 'No, sir,' he said. 'That we cannot do.'

Another great peal of thunder rocked the castle.

Mr. Palfrey stood panting with rage. He could not fire them all. And he longed for their admiration and respect.

He forced a laugh. 'I was a trifle overset,' he said with a ghastly grin. 'Get to your room, Felicity. I shall talk about this later.'

Felicity flew up the stairs, straight to the

nursery, where she threw herself against Miss Chubb's well-upholstered bosom, and cried her eyes out. At long last, she calmed down and gave Miss Chubb the whole story.

'I have no hope,' said Felicity with a pathetic little sob. 'No hope at all.'

'I have been talking to John Tremayne in your absence,' said Miss Chubb. 'We have a plan. We are going to run away tonight—you, me and John.'

CHAPTER FIVE

'This is mad. Quite mad,' said Felicity Channing with a shiver. 'How on earth did I agree to such a mad scheme?'

She stood on top of the cliffs, a little way away from the castle, while the wind howled and the thunder crashed and tumbled about the heavens. A blinding sheet of lightning showed a rope tied firmly to a rock. At the end of that rope hung John Tremayne, staging the 'accident.'

Miss Chubb's plan was being put into operation. The governess had been planning it for some time, never really thinking they would do it, until Felicity's distress forced her to turn the dream into reality. The terrible weather conditions were perfect, and they might never again have such a good chance.

Felicity had left a note to say she could not bear to marry the baron and was running away with Miss Chubb and John Tremayne. They had packed one trunk with their clothes and another trunk that John had hurled over the cliff after opening the lid and removing some of the clothes.

They had gone to a part of the cliff that had fallen into the sea, the land broken away by the force of the deluge. John had noticed this section of cliff before and knew it was only a matter of time before it gave way. Before he had let himself down over the cliff, he had dug deep gouges in the earth with his hands to make it look like someone had desperately tried to save themselves. Now he was leaving torn scraps of clothing caught in rocks and bushes on the way down, as well as some of the contents of the trunk.

As abruptly as it had started, the storm stopped, the huge black mass of clouds sailing away overhead on a high wind. The moon shone down.

'Oh, hurry,' breathed Felicity.

But John's head was already appearing back over the cliff's edge. He clambered onto safe ground, untied the rope, and picking up the heavy jewel box, slung it up onto his shoulder. Felicity and Miss Chubb followed behind, carrying the trunk with their clothes between them.

Felicity and Miss Chubb were dressed in

their men's disguises. The going over the soggy, uneven ground was rough, and Felicity was beginning to wish they had thrown this trunk over the cliff as well when they came to a carriage and horses, hidden behind a thick stand of trees.

'Where did you get this carriage, John?' whispered Felicity, trying to stop her teeth from chattering.

'I went over to Baxeter and bought the lot. I gave a false name, of course.'

'But where did you get the money?'

'Miss Chubb's savings,' said John.

'So, you had all this planned for some time,' said Felicity.

'Don't talk,' said John urgently. 'Get in the carriage.'

Felicity and Miss Chubb climbed in. The carriage dipped and swayed as John climbed up on the box.

'Where are we going?' asked Felicity as the carriage moved off.

'Falmouth,' said Miss Chubb. 'It is at Falmouth that you take up your new identity.'

'New . . . ? Miss Chubb, you had better start at the beginning and tell me what you and John have planned.'

'Well, it's like this,' said Miss Chubb, her voice sounding oddly youthful and excited. 'Although I hoped the baron might not prove to be too terrible, I heard no good of him at all. I remembered how you said we could escape with the jewels, but we would always be hunted and not be able to live openly, even though Mr. Palfrey did not know we had them. So John and I decided that if we could get you to London, and give you a new identity—one that would be grand enough, and would allow you to sell the jewels openly to the best jewelers—you could have a Season and find a gentleman to suit you.'

'And who am I going to be?'

'Princess of Brasnia.'

'That is ridiculous. There is no such place.'

'There is now,' said Miss Chubb cheerfully, 'for I have just invented it. I used to attend the London Season in the old days with my charges, before I came here to work for the Channings. It always struck me as odd that English society was almost ignorant of geography. So, you are now Princess Felicity of Miadaslav, which everyone knows is the capital of Brasnia, and I am your companion, Madame Chubiski.'

'We'll never get away with it,' said Felicity, wondering whether to laugh or cry.

'Rich people can get away with anything,' said Miss Chubb cynically. 'I have enough of my life's savings left to make a good show of it in Falmouth. You see, in our disguises, we arrive at the best inn, The Pelican. We say we are the menservants of the princess. She has just arrived in the country, and we demand the best rooms and a private parlor. Once in our rooms, we take off our disguises and put on our best clothes, and you, my dear, drape yourself in some of the showiest of the jewels. We stay two nights and then begin our journey to London—a slow, triumphal progress. By the time we arrive, everyone will know of our coming. Also, everyone will know that the princess did not come with money but with a great quantity of jewels, which she will trade from time to time.'

'I feel sick,' said Felicity dismally. 'What if I am exposed as a fraud? I shall leave my head on a chopping block at the Tower.'

'Now, that is only for impersonating an English peer or pretending to be any member of the English aristocracy,' said Miss Chubb comfortably. 'The only way you could face prosecution is by using a fake title to get money out of people, which of course you will not do.'

'I don't like it,' murmured Felicity. 'Good heavens! Lord Arthur Bessamy and his friend, Mr. Godolphin. What if I should meet them? They will recognize me.'

'You just stare at them haughtily and ask them why they are insulting you by suggesting you might be some country girl. Besides, the whole country will know of our deaths tomorrow. By the time the Season has begun, everyone will have forgotten about us—even Lord Arthur.'

'But Lord Arthur struck me as being clever.

I am sure he will know there is no such place as Brasnia.'

'Nonsense! I assure you the English aristocracy cannot even point out on the globe the places they visited during the Grand Tour.'

'But what . . . ?'

'Miss Felicity,' interrupted Miss Chubb sternly. 'Do you want to marry the baron?'

'Oh, no,' said Felicity. She sat nervously biting her fingernails, a most unladylike habit, as she worried about her future. But even if the masquerade should only last a short time, what fun she might have. What independence!

In the darkness of the carriage, Felicity began to smile. 'Madame Chubiski,' she said, 'you are a wonder!'

'I have a very vivid imagination,' said Miss Chubb ruefully. 'Anyway, let us try to get some sleep before we arrive at Falmouth.'

Dawn was gilding cobbles of the town of Falmouth when John Tremayne brought the carriage to a halt outside The Pelican.

'Here we go,' muttered Miss Chubb.

Felicity could only stand by and listen in amazement as Miss Chubb, a hat pulled down to conceal most of her face, began to show a previously hidden talent as an actress. In heavily accented English, she grandly set about turning The Pelican on its ears.

The landlord, dazed at this unexpected visit of foreign royalty, set his servants running hither and thither. After all the fuss had died down and the best rooms had been prepared, he positioned himself in the yard to await the arrival of the princess. He was taken aback when Miss Chubb appeared, still in her male disguise, to tell him that the princess had slipped quietly into the inn during all the fuss, but would be prepared to give the landlord an audience, and thank him personally for all his efforts.

The landlord, Mr. Jem Peters, was told to attend the princess in half an hour.

Upstairs, as Miss Chubb darted in and hurriedly began to change into clothes suitable for a royal companion, Felicity threw open the lid of the iron box and blinked as diamonds, rubies, emeralds, sapphires, and gold flashed up at her.

'Oh, my goodness,' said Miss Chubb. 'What jewels! But we can admire them later. Put on the most showy, Miss Felicity, and quickly. The landlord will be here very soon.'

Mr. Peters eventually scratched timidly at the door. John Tremayne answered it, hoping the landlord would not notice that the princess's attendant was wearing outdoor livery.

But the dazed landlord had eyes only for the little figure who sat on a chair by the window.

She was wearing a white silk gown. A diamond tiara blazed in her red hair, and a collar of huge diamonds was clasped about her neck. A rope of real pearls hung down to her waist and a yellow silk sash across her bosom was decorated with a large diamond and ruby brooch in the shape of a cross, which looked very much like an order.

'We are pleassed to thank you,' said Felicity in what she hoped was a foreign accent. 'It ees varry comfortable here.'

'Your Royal Highness,' stammered Mr. Peters. 'My humble inn is entirely at your service.'

Felicity smiled and gave a stately little nod, and John Treymayne held the door open again to indicate that the brief audience was over.

Mr. Peters shot down the stairs, pausing only to grab his hat. The mayor must know of this, and the aldermen.

The beauty of this little princess spread like wildfire. All the long day, Felicity gave audiences, and feeling very guilty, received presents of flowers, fans, trinkets, bales of cloth, gloves, and even baskets of delicacies. She felt even more guilty when the mayor, in his full dress of office, bowed low before her and begged her to let the town of Falmouth have the honor of paying her stay at the inn.

But no one seemed to have the least interest in this mysterious country called Brasnia. No one even wanted to know on which ship the royal party had arrived. Felicity bowed and smiled, and accepted more presents, wondering what on earth was happening back at Tregarthan Castle, and if the infuriating

Lord Arthur Bessamy ever even thought of her.

*   *   *

Lord Arthur Bessamy had slept badly. He had a nagging ache inside, which he put down to indigestion. The food at dinner had been abominable. The noise of the storm had been horrible. He found himself hoping Miss Felicity's boldness and courage ran to coping with storms, and the next minute damned her under his breath.

The ancient chambermaid creaked in and placed a small tray with a cup of weak chocolate beside the bed, and then drew back the curtains at the windows. Sunlight flooded the room. A fine day, thought Lord Arthur, clasping his hands behind his head and staring up at the frayed canopy. A good day for a ride to Tregarthan Castle. It was only decent, he told himself, to make every effort to dissuade Mr. Palfrey from forcing his young stepdaughter into marriage.

A flash of light on the canopy above his head caught his eye. He was just looking curiously at it and wondering what it could be, when the canopy gave way and a flood of water cascaded down all over his body.

He leapt from the bed with a yell. The roof had been leaking during the night, and the rainwater had formed a sort of lake on top of the canopy. Enough was enough. Dolph could stay if he liked, but he, Lord Arthur, was going to go straight to The Green Dolphin, after visiting Tregarthan Castle, and book a room.

Dolph, it transpired, had also suffered a similar disaster during the night, except that the flood had been in the closet where his clothes were hung. They had been dried in the kitchen at a scorching fire and most of them had shrunk.

He was a tubby pathetic figure at the breakfast table, with his waistcoat somewhere up about his chest, and his breeches strained to the point of indecency over his fat thighs.

He gloomily agreed to leave with Lord Arthur, although he tried to protest over the proposed visit to Tregarthan Castle. Miss Channing, pointed out Dolph, had seemed well able to look after herself, and it was folly to interfere in another family's affairs.

But the glory of the day when they finally set out on the road, after leaving a note for the still-sleeping baron, restored both men's spirits. The air was full of lark song, and clouds of little blue butterflies performed their erratic ballet over the strips of fields.

'I didn't really want his money all that much,' said Dolph.

'He may still leave it to you.'

'Not if you succeed in putting an end to this proposed marriage, he won't,' pointed out Dolph.

'I hadn't thought of that,' said Lord Arthur, nodding as a laborer at the side of the road saluted them. 'Better write and tell him it was nothing to do with you.'

'On a sunny day like this, it all seems rather grimy—waiting for someone to pop off to get their moneybags.'

Lord Arthur smiled but did not reply. He slowed as they approached a farmer driving a cart and asked the man if they were on the right road to Tregarthan Castle. It turned out they only had a mile to go.

Soon the fantastic turrets of the castle rose above the moorland.

'What a place!' exclaimed Dolph. 'Like something out of one of those romances. I wonder if they have ghosts.'

'If they have, they must be very modern ones. The castle is a folly I believe, and quite new.'

They bowled across the drawbridge under the portcullis, which glittered wickedly above their heads in the bright sunlight. 'I wonder if it works,' said Dolph, staring up at it. 'I wouldn't want that thing to come crashing down on my head.'

The inner courtyard was empty. No servant came running to hold the horses or to announce their arrival.

Lord Arthur and Dolph got down and tethered the horses to a post and then rang the huge bell that stood beside the brass-bound door.

After some time, the door creaked open. Anderson, the butler, stood looking at them sorrowfully.

'Lord Arthur Bessamy and Mr. Godolphin present their compliments to Mr. Palfrey and wish to speak to him,' said Lord Arthur.

The butler bowed, turned, and walked away. After some hesitation, the two men walked into the hall.

The butler disappeared into a room at the end of the hall. There came the murmur of voices, and then they could hear Mr. Palfrey's voice suddenly sharp and querulous, saying, 'Get rid of them, The disgrace of it all. They must not know.'

Lord Arthur raised his thin black brows. 'Now, what is it that we must not know? Come, Dolph.' And with Dolph following at his heels, he walked straight into the room from which they had heard Mr. Palfrey's voice emerging.

Mr. Palfrey let out an outraged squawk at the sight of them.

'Gentlemen,' he said, shredding a handkerchief between his fingers, 'normally I would be delighted to entertain you, but I am not well, not well at all.'

'We are in fact come to call on Miss Channing.'

'Sleeping,' said Mr. Palfrey. 'Can't be disturbed.'

And then they heard cries from the

90

courtyard and the sound of many feet.

All of them stood stock still, waiting. A group of servants entered with a man in gamekeeper's dress heading them.

'It's terrible, Mr. Palfrey,' said the gamekeeper. 'Just terrible.'

'Let me just see these gentlemen off the premises,' began Mr. Palfrey, but one of the servants behind the gamekeeper cried out, 'They be dead. All of them. Miss Felicity, Miss Chubb, and John Tremayne.'

Like a puppet with its strings cut, Mr. Palfrey dropped into a chair. 'You must be mistaken,' he gasped. 'Where? How?'

The gamekeeper took over. 'We went to look for them like you told us to, seeing as how Miss Felicity had run away, her not wanting to marry the baron.' Mr. Palfrey waved his hands in a despairing way, and turned a ghastly smile on Lord Arthur as if to imply that the gamekeeper was talking nonsense.

'We come to a bit o' the cliff along to the north,' went on the gamekeeper, 'and where the cliff had fallen into the sea during the storm, we found where they'd fallen over.'

'I must see this. I cannot believe it,' babbled Mr. Palfrey, now too overset to worry about Lord Arthur.

They parted to let Mr. Palfrey through, and Lord Arthur and Dolph followed close behind.

As they walked along the cliff, Dolph found himself muttering prayers. If only it were not true. Lord Arthur was clay-white, and his face was set in stern lines.

It was too beautiful a day for tragedy, thought Dolph, in a sort of dazed wonder. The sun still shone, the birds still sang, and the air was sweet with the smell of salt and wildflowers. Tufts of sea pinks grew along the top of the cliff; looking almost shocking in the gaiety of their summer display.

Finally the party came to a halt.

'Look,' said the gamekeeper.

Mr. Palfrey, Lord Arthur, and Dolph looked at the jagged, broken cliff, and the pathetic marks of hands that had clawed into the mud.

'And look down!' cried the gamekeeper. They edged to the broken lip of the cliff. There was a dry bit of turf to the side of the mud. The three men lay down and looked over.

A piece of blue muslin, as blue as the sky above, was caught on a jagged rock halfway down above the foaming sea.

'That was the dress she was wearing,' said Lord Arthur in a bleak voice. 'She was wearing a blue gown when we saw her.'

As they watched, a boat nosed round an outcrop of rock far below. The men in it were scanning the water. One of them cried out, and they put their grappling irons over the side.

'Oh, no,' muttered Dolph. 'I'm going to be sick.'

But they watched as the grappling irons

took hold. A black thing was being pulled up out of the water. It was a trunk with limp, soaking clothes dangling over the side. The men hauled it on board and continued their search.

Still they lay there and watched and watched as the men below searched the restless waves.

At last Mr. Palfrey got shakily to his feet. 'It had nothing to do with me!' he cried. 'It was not my fault.'

A crowd of locals had gathered. As Dolph and Lord Arthur got to their feet as well, one of the yeoman farmers, a free man whose lands did not depend on Mr. Palfrey, bent down and picked up a clod of earth and threw it straight at Mr. Palfrey.

'Murderer!' he cried.

'Stop them,' shouted Mr. Palfrey to his servants, as more missiles followed.

But his servants stood in a circle, staring at him with accusing eyes.

With a frightened little cry, Mr. Palfrey set off running, as stones and turf whistled about his ears.

Dolph reached up and put a plump hand on his friend's shoulder. 'Come away, Arthur,' he said. 'There is nothing we can do for the girl now.'

*   *   *

While Mr. Palfrey was fleeing back to the castle, it was still early morning in Williamsburg, Virginia, and Bessie Redhill was at last up for sale. It had been a nightmare of a voyage, as they were driven off their course time after time by storms and gales. Then the good ship *Mary Bess* had limped into Bermuda for repairs and to take on fresh water before finally setting off south for Virginia.

For a good part of the journey Bessie had hung between life and death. She had been suffering from severe concussion, as well as from the overdose of laudanum; she had been violently seasick and then had contracted a fever. She sometimes thought that the only thing keeping her alive was her burning thirst for revenge. Before she had come down with the fever, she had begged a scrap of oilskin from one of the crew and had sewn that precious will up in it. She had not confided in the captain. The captain was an accomplice of Mr. Palfrey's in her eyes.

Virginia was about the worst place where she could have been sold. The decline of white servitude had begun some twenty years earlier because of the vast numbers of black slaves. Why buy a white, who must be granted his or her freedom and paid wages in seven years' time, when a black worked for nothing for life? White servants were rated cheap, and their masters often tried by various ruses to prolong their servitude. In other states, Connecticut, for instance, there were no laws under which a runaway could be recovered. But there were such laws in Virginia and a recaptured servant could have years added onto that seven-year term.

At least Williamsburg was far better than anything Bessie had expected. She had imagined with dread a wild and barren land. A former governor, Francis Nicholson, had planned 'a green country town.' Williamsburg was divided into half-acre lots on which dwellings were set back, by law, six feet from the street. The impression was one of prettiness, elegance, and cleanliness.

Bessie, standing on the auction block, envied the Scottish servants. Provided they had a clan name like Macleod or Macdonald, one of their American clansmen would buy them on the spot and set them free.

She was too tired and dazed to really know what was happening. The fierce heat on her uncovered head was making the colorful scene swim before her eyes.

'Get down, Redhill. You're took,' barked the auctioneer. Numbly, Bessie stepped down.

A black manservant in neat livery said, 'Follow me. Mistress is waiting in the carriage.'

Bessie stumbled after him through the crowd.

A lady was sitting in an open carriage. 'This servant shall travel with me, Peter,' she said to the servant.

The manservant opened the carriage door and, catching the eye of his mistress, helped Bessie in.

'I am Mrs. Harrington,' said the lady, unfurling her parasol. 'Walk on, Peter.' The carriage moved off.

'I must make one thing clear . . . Bessie, is it not? I am the wife of the Reverend Hereward Harrington. We do not believe in slavery. You will commence your duties as a kitchen maid until you are trained in our ways and may rise to a better position. You will be paid wages and you may, as from this moment, consider yourself a free woman.'

'Thank you,' whispered Bessie, tears of weakness and relief beginning to roll down her cheeks.

'You poor woman. You will be nursed back to health before you start your duties. Now, do not try to talk. Here, take this parasol, and keep the sun from your head.'

Bessie looked into Mrs. Harrington's kind eyes and then at the saucy silk parasol with the ivory handle that she was holding out to her, and for the first time in her life, Bessie Redhill began to believe in the existence of a merciful God.

*   *   *

Dolph had felt more cheerful the next day after a good dinner and an excellent night's sleep on a comfortable bed at The Green Dolphin. But his feeling of well-being did not last long. It transpired that Lord Arthur had rented a rowing boat and expected his friend to accompany him to help in the grim search for the bodies.

The sea was mercifully calm, but the landswell was enough to make Dolph begin to wish he had not dined so well. Hatless and in his shirt-sleeves, Lord Arthur rested on the oars for a moment.

'One of the fishermen told me, Dolph, that bodies are often swept out to sea. I fear they may end up in France.'

'In that case . . .' said Dolph hopefully.

'But we shall continue our search. Perhaps a little farther out.' Lord Arthur began to pull away from the cliffs with powerful strokes.

Lord Arthur was the youngest son of the Duke of Pentshire. He was very rich. All of which, thought Dolph queasily, should have made the noble lord remember what was due his position. He should have hired men to search and men to row.

'There's something white in the water,' shouted Lord Arthur suddenly, making Dolph jump. 'Over on the port side.'

Dolph looked over to his left and saw a white shape bobbing on the water. 'Oh, dear,' he moaned.

'Get the grappling iron,' ordered Lord Arthur, shipping the oars.

Dolph closed his eyes while Lord Arthur fished in the water. When he opened them again, Lord Arthur was standing in the rocking boat, looking thoughtfully at a sopping white dress on the end of the iron. 'More clothes,' he murmured.

He took the dress off the iron and then sat down in the boat, shook it, and held it up. It had been a pretty little dress with a flounced yoke and a flounced hem.

'How tall would you say Miss Channing was?' asked Lord Arthur.

'Little under my height,' said Dolph, surprised. ' 'Bout five foot four inches, I would guess.'

Lord Arthur studied the dress again, and then looked thoughtfully at the cliff.

'You know what puzzles me, Dolph,' he said. 'Clothes have been found. But you would have expected trinkets to have been lying down on the cliff, or floating about—fans and ribbons, shoes and laces.' He picked up the oars and began to row powerfully back in the direction of the little harbor below the village.

'Where are we going?' asked Dolph.

'Back to Tregarthan Castle. I want a look at that trunk that was recovered.'

'Why?'

'Oh, just an idea.'

When they got to the castle, it was to find that the portcullis was indeed a working one, for it was firmly down at the end of the drawbridge.

'Mr. Palfrey must be frightened of a hanging,' said Lord Arthur.

There was a bell beside the portcullis of the same size as the one beside the front door. He gave it an energetic peal and waited until a servant ran out to answer its summons.

'I was to let no one through, my lord,' said the servant, 'and Mr. Palfrey is lying down, having taken a sleeping draft.'

'I merely want to examine the trunk of clothes that was found yesterday,' said Lord Arthur. 'Raise this silly contraption immediately.'

He and Dolph waited while the servant ran to fetch three of his fellows, and it took the combined efforts of the four to winch up the portcullis.

Anderson, on hearing their strange request, turned them over to the housekeeper, Mrs. Jessop, who took them up to Felicity's bedchamber.

'I had not the heart to take the clothes out and wash them,' said Mrs. Jessop, beginning to cry.

'Do not distress yourself,' said Lord Arthur. 'Leave us for a little. We shall take our leave shortly.'

Watched by Dolph, Lord Arthur carefully took items out of the trunk and studied them. Two strangely small dresses, an old pair of shoes, an ugly tartan scarf, four old bonnets—

not the sort of styles one would expect the modish Miss Channing to wear.

A slow smile curled Lord Arthur's lips. Then he began to laugh.

Dolph looked at his friend in shock and outrage.

'Have you gone mad?' he cried.

'No, no, my friend,' said Lord Arthur. 'I fear the tragedy has overset my nerves.' He put the clothes back in the trunk, slammed down the lid and left the room, with Dolph trotting at his heels. Grief took people in very strange ways, thought Dolph.

*   *   *

Princess Felicity of Brasnia made a triumphal exit from the town of Falmouth. The mayor bowed and a military band played a brisk march. Felicity waved graciously until the people and the town were left behind.

'Thank goodness that is over,' said Felicity, leaning back with her head against the squabs. 'It is amazing, this business of being a princess. No one will let us pay for anything. I feel such a fraud.'

'They all enjoyed themselves,' said Miss Chubb. 'But the one thing now troubling me is our lack of servants. It will look odd if we do not hire some. You have only John. And, oh, how difficult it will be with a retinue of servants. We shall have to play our parts even in our sleep.

'Perhaps our John will think of something,' continued Miss Chubb. 'He is proving to be amazingly clever.'

'Well, at least I can take this heavy tiara and collar off for a little,' sighed Felicity. 'Do you really think Mr. Palfrey will believe us dead?'

'Bound to,' said Miss Chubb bracingly. 'It all went off splendidly.'

Felicity frowned. 'I am a little worried about the things we left in that trunk that went over the cliff. I put in some of my gowns that I had not worn since I was about thirteen. But I could not bear to throw away my lovely new clothes—you know, the ones Mr. Palfrey ordered from London to make me look attractive to the baron.'

'But you did sacrifice the nicest one, the blue one that John tore a piece from and left on that rock.'

'So I did,' said Felicity cheerfully, 'and no one would think for a moment that I would deliberately destroy such a lovely gown as that.

'As far as Mr. Palfrey is concerned, I must be as dead as mutton. I am glad I wrote to my sisters from Falmouth to tell them the truth—only not the bit about my going to London as a princess—only that I am alive and will soon be in touch with them. They will not betray me to Mr. Palfrey.'

Now it was Miss Chubb's turn to look worried. 'Even when they do not find the bodies, there will be some sort of service, and your sisters, bless them, are none of them actresses. Mr. Palfrey may notice their lack of grief.'

'Not he,' said Felicity. 'He will be so busy covering up his own lack of grief that he will not notice how anyone else is behaving!'

CHAPTER SIX

They were waiting in the wings, waiting to go on stage, waiting for the Season to begin.

London's curiosity about this new princess had not yet been satisfied. Princess Felicity's servants had announced to all callers that Her Majesty had no intentions of meeting any social engagements until the start of the Season.

Felicity wanted to be well prepared and to have her servants thoroughly coached. For very few of them were real servants. On their journey to London, John Tremayne had sought out the local candidates for the 'royal' household. All, except the butler, had been found guilty of minor crimes, usually caused by near-starvation. The promise of a good home, wages, and an escape from prison had bound them all to secrecy. But they had to be trained. Housemaids and chambermaids were easily dealt with. The cook, a motherly widow whose only crime had been to steal a loaf of bread, had to have time to learn to produce large banquets, and she, in turn, had to train the kitchen staff. The butler, an ex-burglar turned religious maniac, had been chosen by John, who had found him emerging from prison after having served his sentence. That he had not been hanged was a miracle. It was his appearance that had struck John immediately. He was fat and pompous and had a cold and quelling eye. Apart from the fact that the new butler, Mr. Spinks, was apt to treat John Tremayne as if he were an angel specially sent down from heaven to rescue him, Spinks studied his new duties assiduously and soon showed a talent for running the household. He was apt to fall to his knees and pray loudly when upset, but so very little upset him these days that Felicity felt they could well put up with this little eccentricity.

They had been very lucky. They had not even had to search for a town house. On their journey toward London, a lord who had heard of their arrival in his area had promptly offered them the hospitality of his country mansion, and, on their departure, had insisted they take the keys to his town house in Chesterfield Gardens, Mayfair, saying that he did not intend to visit London during the next Season, and the house would otherwise be standing empty.

John Tremayne found illiteracy an

increasing disadvantage and so, with Felicity's permission, he visited the Fleet Prison until he found a suitable schoolmaster, paid his debts, brought him back to Chesterfield Gardens, and set him up as resident tutor. The schoolmaster's name was Mr. Paul Silver. He was a thin, scholastic gentleman in his fifties with a head of beautifully fine, silver hair to match his name.

Felicity and Miss Chubb often donned their men's disguises and went out to walk about London and stare in awe at all the marvelous goods in the shop windows. After the quiet of the Cornish coast, London was a bewildering kaleidoscope of movement and color and noise. Light curricles and phaetons darted here and there like elegant boats surmounting the rapids of the London streets. Heavy stagecoaches rumbled along Piccadilly, but even their majestic sound was almost drowned out by the grumbling roar of the brewers' sledges and the government lottery sledges, grating over the cobbled streets. Carts piled high with fruit and vegetables from the nurseries of Kensington headed through the West End on their way to Covent Garden market.

Then there were so many varieties of street performers. Felicity saw, after walking along only a very short stretch of Oxford Street, a man with a dancing bear and a drum; an organ grinder with his monkey perched on his shoulder; a man with a trumpet announcing in a hoarse voice between fanfares that a six-headed cow could be seen for only two pennies; a pretty girl in a spangled dress who danced to a tambourine; and three acrobats throwing one another about.

It was all this whirling excitement of being in the capital that eased Felicity's guilty conscience. The boredom of those long, empty days in Mr. Palfrey's scrubbed and polished castle seemed even more horrible in retrospect than even Mr. Palfrey himself. She had not read the newspapers but had gathered from Mr. Silver, the tutor, who read most of them, that the story of her 'death' had even reached the London papers, with a subsequent short paragraph saying that a memorial service had been held, during which Mr. Palfrey had been seen to weep copiously. 'More onions,' thought Felicity cynically.

The famous London jewelers, Rundell and Bridge, had heard of Princess Felicity. Not only had they bought some of the jewels for a fair sum, but had embarrassed Felicity dreadfully by sending her a present of an exquisite turquoise and gold necklace. She had had a dressmaker's dummy made of her figure and sent to the top dressmakers. Felicity did not want them to call at Chesterfield Gardens and gossip about herself and her staff until she felt they were all coached and ready for closer scrutiny.

But as the novelty of London began to die down, Felicity would often find herself thinking of Lord Arthur. He was thirty-one, she discovered, and had never married. Although he had the reputation of being a hardened bachelor, it evidently did not deter the debutantes and their mamas from hoping that one day he would drop the handkerchief. She knew she was bound to meet him during the forthcoming Season, and that thought sent little shivers of anticipation through her body.

It was Mr. Silver's job, apart from his teaching duties, to study the social columns and compile a list for Felicity of all the people she ought to entertain, along with a list of eligible bachelors.

She was looking down the latest list he had compiled one day when she said with a little laugh, 'I see a Mr. Charles Godolphin here. I have met him and I hope to goodness he does not recognize me and only thinks the similarity in looks between the princess and a certain Miss Channing is extraordinary. But I see no mention of his friend, Lord Arthur Bessamy.'

'Ah, no,' said Mr. Silver, reaching for a pair of steel-rimmed spectacles and popping them on his nose. 'Let me see . . . I have my old lists somewhere about. I struck him off about a month ago. Yes. Here we are. Lord Arthur Bessamy became engaged to Miss Martha Barchester of Hapsmere Manor in Suffolk.'

'I would have thought,' said Felicity in a

voice that to her own surprise trembled a little, 'that Lord Arthur would never marry.'

'So did everyone else,' said Mr. Silver. 'There is a piece about him here. I find the more scandalous newspapers a great source of information. He bought a place near Hapsmere Manor last winter. You see, as the younger son of a duke, he has money but no responsibilities or lands, and heretofore evidently lived only in town. But he appears to have decided to settle in the country. The Barchesters are his neighbors. A very suitable marriage. The Barchesters are a very old family—Norman, I believe.' He broke off and looked up in surprise. Felicity had gone.

Felicity went quickly to her room and put on her male disguise. Then she slipped out of the house and walked rapidly in the direction of Hyde Park. A pale sun was shining, and the air was sweet with the heavy smell of hawthorn blossom. It was the fashionable hour, and carriages flew past round the ring with their elegant occupants, the ladies wearing the thinnest of muslins despite the chill of the spring day.

She stood watching them, thinking she did not really belong anywhere. She would never return to Tregarthan Castle, and yet she felt she did not belong in this world of giggling, overly sensitive ladies who practiced how to faint with as much assiduity as they practiced the pianoforte. And the men, with their flicking handkerchiefs and their fussy mannerisms, their rouged faces and cynical assessing eyes, repelled her.

And then a thought struck Felicity, a thought that seemed to lighten her depression. 'I do not need to marry. I can enjoy one Season, go to all the balls and parties, and perhaps even see the Prince Regent. And then I can sell some more jewels, and dear Miss Chubb and I can retire somewhere quiet in the country and settle down.' It was a very comforting thought, and only a little nagging wonder about this Miss Barchester came into her mind to diffuse that comfort. What was she like, this paragon, who had succeeded where so many others had failed?

*　　*　　*

Miss Martha Barchester was like a Byzantine ivory. She had a long, thin, calm face and a long, thin, flat-chested body. Her thick brown hair was parted at the center and combed back into two wings to frame her white face. She was twenty-nine years old. Even her parents wondered what it was about this rather terrifying daughter of theirs that had attracted Lord Arthur.

It had taken a magic potion to make Titania wake from her sleep and fall in love with an ass. But at a certain stage in their lives, even the most hardened rakes and confirmed bachelors need no magic to make them fall in love with the first woman they see. All at once, they are simply hit with an overwhelming desire to get married. The period is usually brief and violent, and they usually emerge from it to find themselves married to a woman they do not know the first thing about.

And so it was with Lord Arthur. First had come the desire for a home and lands. Those being acquired, it followed that he must have a hostess for his home, and a mother for his heirs.

He had to confess to himself that he thought very often about Felicity Channing. He felt he had escaped from the folly that can often lead gentlemen of mature years to propose to chits barely out of the schoolroom. Perhaps the attraction Miss Barchester held for him was that she was everything Felicity was not. She was cool and poised, and never made a sudden or hurried movement or appeared to be swayed by any vulgar emotion whatsoever.

Farming was Lord Arthur's new interest and consuming passion. He felt it would be wonderful to return in the evenings to such a calm and stately creature as Miss Barchester. Their wedding was to take place the following year in the local church. On the acceptance of his proposal, Lord Arthur had taken Miss Barchester in his arms and kissed her. Her kiss had been cool, and her lips had been tightly compressed. But because his physical outdoors activities had taken care of his more earthy feelings, Lord Arthur saw nothing wrong in her virginal response. Ladies were not expected to be passionate anyway.

Dolph, calling on a visit a week before the Season was due to begin, thought his friend looked remarkably well—healthy, happy, and a trifle pompous. Lord Arthur drove him out round the estates and the village, and everywhere forelocks were tugged by men, and women curtsied.

'Quite feudal down here,' remarked Dolph, privately thinking that all this adulation was not doing his rather arrogant friend one little bit of good. 'Don't know but what I don't prefer that independent lot down in Cornwall.'

'Cornwall!' said Lord Arthur sharply. 'Have you been there recently?'

'No, never been back,' said Dolph, casting Lord Arthur a sideways glance. 'M'uncle wrote to say he was crushed down with that girl, Felicity Channing's death, although I suppose it's only the gout as usual. Seems Mr. Palfrey has restored his reputation. Of late he's had whole fleets of boats dragging all around the coast for a sign of the bodies.'

'Dear me,' said Lord Arthur. 'Left it a bit late, hasn't he?'

'Well, he says he won't rest until Felicity has had a Christian burial. The locals say he must have been fond of her after all.'

'I wonder,' said Lord Arthur.

'Talking of Miss Felicity, I had the most awful shock t'other week.'

'See a ghost?'

'Yes, how did you guess! Have you heard of the Princess Felicity of Brasnia?'

'Of where? My dear Dolph, there is no such country.'

'There is. Everyone's heard of it. Somewhere around Russia.' Dolph waved a chubby hand to the east. 'As I was saying, all London has been abuzz with talk of this princess. You know, her beauty is said to be rare and her jewels magnificent. She has been in residence all winter, but no one had seen her. But last week, she went out driving for the first time. What a sensation! People fighting and screaming to get a look at her. At first, I didn't see her face, I was so knocked back with the idea of someone wearing a diamond tiara in the middle of Hyde Park during the day. Then I looked at her properly and nearly dropped down in a faint. I could swear I was looking at Miss Felicity Channing.'

Lord Arthur let the reins drop, and the horses slowed to an amble. 'And . . .?' he prompted.

'I rode straight up to her carriage and, like a fool, I cried, "Miss Felicity! You are alive!" She had one of those double glasses, and she raised it at me and looked at me with such hauteur that I nearly sank. "You were saying somezink?" she asked, and of course, I realized all at once it was not Miss Felicity at all. How could it be? I stammered out my apologies, and she bowed her beautiful little head with those fantastic diamonds flashing and burning, and she said, "We are giffink a rout on the tenth. You come?" I gave her my card and swore that nothing would keep me away. I'm the envy of all the fellows. Everyone desperately fighting to see if they can get an invite, sending presents and poems, and lying in wait outside her door. Duffy Gordon-Pomfret even slept on her doorstep, but her butler, a most odd man, came out, shook him awake, read him the parable of the talents, then told him if he had nothing better to do with his time, he might be better employed in finding a job of work. Work!' said Dolph, shaking his head in amazement.

'I would like to attend that rout,' said Lord Arthur slowly.

'I'm sure you would,' said Dolph gleefully. 'But you can't. All of London wants to get through her door.'

'When did you plan to return to London?'

'Well, unless you're going to throw me out, I meant to get back around the eighth to collect a new suit of evening clothes from the tailor.'

'Call on Princess Felicity,' said Lord Arthur, 'and tell her your friend, Lord Arthur Bessamy, wishes to meet her, and see what she says. I shall take you back to London myself.'

112

Dolph looked huffy. It was not often he was invited to a rout from which his rich and elegant friend was excluded. Then his face lightened. 'I'll ask,' he said cheerfully. 'But she's bound to refuse. Now, when am I to meet your beloved?'

'If you mean Miss Barchester, then say so,' said Lord Arthur curtly. 'This afternoon, at four, for tea.'

Dolph could not believe his eyes when he was introduced to Miss Barchester. He thought she looked as if one of the marble statues on the terrace of her home had come to life. She even had thick white eyelids and a small thin-lipped curved smile.

Lord Arthur, teacup in hand, was standing by the fireplace talking to Mr. Barchester. Mr. Barchester was a plump, rounded man with a jolly face, and his wife, dressed in chintz, looked like an overstuffed sofa. How two such cheerful individuals could have produced the pale and chilly Martha Barchester was beyond Dolph. He found that lady was eyeing him with a gray, cold look. Her gaze dropped from his face and fastened on the area of shirt that was bulging out from under his waistcoat. Dolph always felt his clothes took on a nasty life of their own the minute they left the hands of his valet. His waistcoats tried to move up to his chin, his shirts separated themselves from his breeches, the strings at the knees of his breeches untied themselves, and the starch left all his cravats a bare half an hour after he had put them on.

His teacup rattled in the saucer as Miss Barchester began to speak. 'Our fashions become more extreme, do you not think, Mr. Godolphin?'

'I . . . I . . .' bleated Dolph.

'Yes, it is bad enough when the ladies adopt styles of semi-nudity and wear their waistlines up around their armpits. Now, *I* have my waistline in the right place. I never follow fashion. Fashion follows *me*.'

'Indeed,' said Dolph. 'I fear London fashion cannot have had a chance to see you, Miss Barchester, for all the ladies adopt the high waistline.'

'Are you contradicting me by any chance, Mr. Godolphin?'

'No, no. I . . .'

'Good. Male fashions are every bit as ridiculous. Why do you think so many men aspire to be Beau Brummells when they do not possess either his air or figure?' Her pale eyes fastened again on Dolph's area of shirt.

'Blessed if I know,' said Dolph crossly.

'London fashions,' pursued Miss Barchester, 'are distasteful to me.'

'Then, it's as well you ain't in London,' pointed out Dolph. He took a swig of tepid tea and eyed her over the rim of his cup.

'But I shall be. I am thinking of persuading Mama and Papa to take me for a few weeks. I aim to . . . how do the vulgar put it? . . . *cut a dash.*'

Dolph looked at her curiously. Could she be funning? Or was her vanity so great that she really thought she could impress society?

But she was his best friend's fiancée. He forced himself to be gallant. 'Well, by Jove, Miss Barchester, the ladies of London will be agog to see the fair charmer who has stolen the heart of such a hardened bachelor as Lord Arthur.'

'Exactly,' said Miss Barchester sweetly.

Dolph blinked in amazement. This engagement to one of the most eligible men in the country had quite gone to Miss Barchester's head. What on earth did Arthur see in the creature?

At that moment Lord Arthur strolled over to join them. 'You are making me jealous, the pair of you,' he teased. 'I saw you, rattling away there like old friends.'

Miss Barchester at his arrival on the scene became quiet and submissive. The wings of her brown hair shone softly in the candlelight, and the smooth drapery of her old-fashioned gown fell in straight lines from her waist to the floor like a medieval garment. She kept her eyes demurely lowered.

'By George!' thought Dolph, alarmed. 'Arthur thinks he's got himself a meek, old-fashioned wife.'

At least Lord Arthur could be counted on

not to ask his friend's opinion of Miss Barchester or discuss her in any way. And that was a mercy. For Dolph knew he would be hard put to it to think of anything good to say about her.

On the road home, he remembered the princess's rout and at the same time decided to do his uttermost to secure Lord Arthur an invitation. Anyone who saw the fairy-tale princess could never look with any complacency on such an antidote as Martha Barchester.

*   *   *

Mr. Palfrey told his butler, Anderson, to tell the boatmen to be ready to set off at dawn the next day. The search must go on.

Anderson bowed and then went off to confide in Mrs. Jessop, not for the first time, that they had been mistaken in Mr. Palfrey. He must have loved Miss Felicity very much the way he searched and searched for her poor body.

Once he had gone, Mr. Palfrey darted to the door of the library and turned the key in the lock. Lovingly, he spread the castle blueprints out on the table before him.

In her haste, Miss Chubb had forgotten to shut the door of the priest's hole properly. Some months after Felicity's 'death,' Mr. Palfrey, in one of his feverish hunts for the

116

jewels, had noticed the crack in the wall and had discovered the hiding place. And that is how he had found the plans. He had searched the priest's hole thoroughly and had found the high ledge and the clean square in the dust that showed that a large box had recently rested on it.

From there he had deduced Felicity must have had the jewels in hiding and had taken them with her. It stood to reason that she would not have dared run away without any money. So the Channing jewels must have gone to the bottom of the ocean and, at least they, unlike the bodies, could not have been carried out to sea.

That was the reason he had the sea under the part of the cliff where they had gone over, searched each day so thoroughly.

He rolled up the plans and decided there were really no more undiscovered hiding places outside the priest's hole and the hidden staircase.

He would go to sleep early so as to be ready to continue the search early in the morning.

As soon as a red stormy dawn lit the heaving gray sea, Mr. Palfrey was there in an open boat piloted by the yeoman who had shied a piece of turf at him, but who now respected this man who had proved his love for the lost girl. Mr. Palfrey had grappling irons and various contrivances for hooking down into the water. It was the lowest tide they had had for some months, and Mr. Palfrey saw with rising excitement that there was an almost uncovered stretch of sand at the base of the rock. 'Over there!' he cried to the yeoman, Mr. Godfrey.

'Better be careful,' shouted Mr. Godfrey as the open boat scraped its keel on the sand. 'Won't be much time.'

'The spade! The spade!' shrieked Mr. Palfrey excitedly to one of the other men. 'No, no. Give it to me. I shall dig myself.'

'Look the way he do dig!' exclaimed Mr. Godfrey. 'He'll cut any corpse in half, spearing down like that.'

They waited patiently, watching Mr. Palfrey's feverish efforts, half-amused, half-touched.

Then Mr. Palfrey felt his spade clink against something. He threw the spade aside, and, kneeling down on the watery strip of sand, began to scrape at it with his fingers.

With a triumphant cry, he held up a necklace. The fierce red sun shone on it and it burned with all the fire of priceless rubies.

Mr. Palfrey gave a hysterical laugh. 'The Channing jewels!' he shouted. 'I have found them. Oh, God, at last. After all these weary days of searching.'

The men in the boat watched him, stricken. 'You mean,' said Mr. Godfrey at last, 'that that's what you was looking for all along? You didn't give a rap for Miss Felicity.'

But Mr. Palfrey, ecstatic with delight, turned

118

the flashing stones this way and that.

Then a cloud covered the red sun. It took all the light out of the day. It took all the fire from the sea.

And the necklace in Mr. Palfrey's hand turned into cheap glass, as if the Cornish pixies had played some hellish trick on him.

He had betrayed himself. The men in the boat looked at him with eyes of stone.

Mr. Godfrey seized the oars and shoved off.

'You can't leave me,' shouted Mr. Palfrey. 'The tide has turned.'

'Then, swim, you liddle ferret,' shouted back Mr. Godfrey.

Mr. Palfrey stood there until the boat had disappeared round the point. Then, shivering and whimpering and cursing Felicity under his breath, he began to swim.

It was as well he remembered the secret staircase—for the castle was under siege by angry locals at the front. It would be a long time before he dared poke his nose out of doors again.

*   *   *

On the eighth of April, Mr. Godolphin had a very odd audience with Princess Felicity of Brasnia. For he did not see her.

He was ushered into a stately drawing room by an unnerving sort of butler who fixed Dolph's tubby figure with a haughty look, and

119

said, 'Make not provision for the flesh to fulfill the lusts thereof,' before bowing and stalking out.

A terrifyingly massive woman, with a hand outstretched, came down the room toward him. She was dressed from head to foot in black velvet. 'I am Madame Chubiski,' she announced.

Dolph bowed. 'I am come to see Her Royal Highness.'

'Vot is eet you vish?' said Madame Chubiski.

'I wish to speak to Princess Felicity about it, if I may.'

'What is it?' came a light young voice from behind a carved screen in the corner. Madame Chubiski waved an imperious hand, and Dolph approached the screen cautiously.

'I am come to beg a favor, ma'am,' he said timidly. Then he thought of Martha Barchester, and his voice strengthened. 'My friend, Lord Arthur Bessamy, would be deeply honored if you could manage to issue him an invitation to your rout.'

There was a long silence, and Dolph felt almost as if the temperature in the room had dropped by several degrees. He turned about and smiled winningly at Madame Chubiski, who glowered back.

At last, the princess's voice came to him very faintly from behind the screen. 'Yes,' it said on a little sigh. 'He may come.'

'Thank you,' said Dolph, bowing to the screen.

'You've got what you want, young man, so take your leave,' growled a robust English accent behind him. Dolph started. But there was still only Madame Chubiski in the room—who had sounded so foreign only a moment before.

But he felt he had better leave quickly before the princess changed her mind.

When he had gone, Miss Chubb said ruefully, 'Did you really have to give him an invitation?'

'Yes, this way Lord Arthur will not suspect anything,' said Felicity, emerging from behind the screen. 'Besides, there will be such a crush, the poor man will have difficulty in seeing me at all! And I am supposed to be dead, remember? You know, Miss Chubb, I am so tired of this silly accent I have to affect, and your own is beginning to come and go alarmingly. Why do we not start to speak proper English—and praise our good Mr. Silver for effecting the transformation?'

'Good idea,' sighed Miss Chubb. 'Do you know, I live in terror of being confronted by some fool who claims to speak Brasnian!'

CHAPTER SEVEN

'I speak excellent Brasnian, Your Royal Highness,' said Lord Arthur Bessamy.

Felicity carefully concealed all the dismay she felt. Miss Chubb had made a dreadful mistake. There must be a wretched place called Brasnia after all. Around them, the glittering cream of London society ebbed and flowed in the pink and gold saloon at Chesterfield Gardens.

With a thin little smile, Felicity said, 'I do not wish to speak Brasnian. It would shame my tutor, who has been at such pains to teach me excellent English.'

'You are a credit to him, ma'am,' said Lord Arthur, smiling down into her eyes. 'One would suppose, to listen to you, that you had been speaking English all of your life.'

Felicity glanced nervously sideways, looking for help. But Lord Arthur was a leader of society and so was being allowed a few moments alone with her, a courtesy afforded to very few. Miss Chubb's tall, feathered headdress could be seen at the far end of the room. 'She should not have left me alone for a minute,' thought Felicity, irritation now mixing with her fear.

She took a deep breath. 'May I congratulate you on your forthcoming marriage, Lord

Arthur?'

'Thank you,' he said stiffly. 'You are well-informed.'

'I make it my business to be so.'

'Tell me, do you know much of our country?'

'No, not much.'

'You have never been to Cornwall, for example?'

'I believe I have.'

Lord Arthur leaned closer to her and murmured, 'Where in Cornwall exactly?'

'Why, I arrived at Falmouth.'

'His Royal Highness, the Prince of Wales, the Prince Regent,' cried Spinks loudly.

Silence fell on the room. The guests parted to form two lines.

Lord Arthur bowed and moved away. Felicity began to shake. This was flying too high! She had not invited the Prince, would not have dreamed of doing so. But Prinny went anywhere in society he wanted to go, invited or not.

How very fat he is, was Felicity's dazed thought as the corpulent royal figure moved toward her.

Miss Chubb tried to edge around the outside of the room to get to Felicity. Why had the Prince come this evening of all evenings? wondered Miss Chubb frantically. It had all been going so splendidly, and there had been no flash of recognition on Lord Arthur's face when he had first seen Felicity. And she looked so young and regal, standing in a white silk gown embroidered with tiny diamonds and seed pearls and with the Channing diamonds glittering and flashing.

Felicity sank into a deep curtsey before the Prince Regent. 'This is a very great honor,' she said.

'On the contrary,' said the Prince, 'it is you who do England honor. We have never been to Brasnia.'

'No, sire?' said Felicity in a shaky voice.

'Can't go anywhere with Boney strangling Europe. Brasnia, now let me see . . . ?'

The color flew from Felicity's cheeks. She was about to be found out.

The Prince shook his heavy head so that the curls of his nut-brown wig bounced and shook. 'We have never heard of the place. Where is it?'

'On th-the R-Russian b-border,' stammered Felicity.

'And your father, King . . . ?'

Felicity closed her eyes in despair. She tried to think up some lie, something to say—anything! But it was as if terror had frozen her brain.

'I fear Princess Felicity is overcome with the heat of the rooms,' came Lord Arthur's voice. 'Let me explain, sire. Brasnia is a small principality, not a kingdom. It is a very small country, about the size of Luxembourg.

Princess Felicity's brother, Prince Georgi, is the ruler.' His voice dropped to a boring monotone. 'It is mainly an agricultural country, growing maize-corn, wheat, and oats in the fertile plains surrounding the River Zorg. The river itself produces excellent fish, one of which is the curpa, a local delicacy that has to be cleaned by experts because it contains a deadly poison. Anyone who is unlucky enough to take this poison endures severe fits of vomiting and the flux prior to death. What is even more peculiar is that the vomit is bright green in color . . .'

'Gad's Oonds!' cried the Prince, holding his fat stomach. 'Enough! Enough! We do not wish to hear another word.'

He nodded curtly to Felicity and hurried away. His voice carried back to Felicity and Lord Arthur. 'What on earth is up with that fellow, Bessamy? Used to be a wit. Now about the biggest bore in Christendom. We are bored. We wish to leave . . .'

The Prince's petulant voice faded away as he disappeared out the door of the saloon with Lord Alvanley at his heels.

Felicity looked up nervously at Lord Arthur. Either he had gone raving mad or he had mistaken Brasnia for another country—or he knew the truth about her. And Felicity was very much afraid he knew the truth.

But he merely smiled, a charming smile that lit up his eyes. 'You must have accepted many social engagements for the weeks to come, ma'am.'

'N-no,' said Felicity breathlessly. 'I mean, I have not accepted any invitations as yet. Madame Chubb . . . iski is going to look through them all and choose which ones we should attend.'

'So, you had not planned to go to the balloon ascension at the Belvedere Tea Gardens in Pentonville tomorrow afternoon?'

'No, my lord.'

'Then, you and . . . er . . . Madame Chubiski must allow me and Mr. Godolphin the pleasure of escorting you there tomorrow at three o'clock.'

'S-so soon? I had planned to stay quietly at home for a few days.'

'Why not, Your Highness? Such poor creatures as myself and Dolph will not be able to come near you once you start the social round. Besides, we could talk about that fascinating country, Brasnia.'

'Yes, we could, couldn't we,' said Felicity miserably. She felt he was teasing her, playing with her. Well, she might as well accept his invitation and learn whether he planned to expose her.

'We shall be pleased to go with you,' she said.

He looked down at the downcast little face under the flashing tiara. 'Then, I shall go and tell Dolph the good news.' He stepped back from her, bowing as he went, but before other guests could close in round Felicity, he suddenly said, 'My goodness. How I have misled our Regent. I was thinking of another country altogether. I fear I had forgotten that I do not know Brasnia at all.'

Felicity looked at him sharply, but could see no guile or mockery on his face.

He bowed again.

At that moment, Miss Chubb finally reached Felicity's side. She hoped nothing had gone wrong. But Felicity was already talking to some of the other guests. She looked relaxed and happy—happier than she had looked all evening. Miss Chubb smiled with relief. For one moment, she had thought Lord Arthur must have said something to upset Felicity, but it was obvious from Felicity's manner that nothing had gone wrong at all.

*   *   *

'No, I shall not wear that wretched tiara again during the day,' said Felicity the following afternoon as she and Miss Chubb made ready for their outing. 'It makes my head ache.'

'But you are supposed to be a princess,' protested Miss Chubb.

'I am sure princesses do not go about encrusted with jewels. Hand me that rope of pearls. They are magnificent enough on their own. And see, I have this pretty straw bonnet ornamented with silk flowers. Surely that is smart enough for an afternoon occasion? Besides, the *Times* has been quite critical over the flamboyance of my dress.' Felicity picked up the newspaper and read, 'PRINCESS FELICITY, DESPITE HER BEAUTY, PORTRAYS A CERTAIN EASTERN EUROPEAN BARBARISM IN HER DRESS. TOO MANY JEWELS CAN ONLY BE CONSIDERED *NOT TASTY*. You see?'

'I suppose so,' said Miss Chubb. 'You seem to have been accepted by everyone. Lord Arthur worries me, however. All that nonsense he told the Prince Regent about Brasnia . . .'

'But I told you, he said he had made a mistake. I thought he might be mocking me, but there was no mockery or teasing in his face. All the same, it is as well to make sure, which is why I have not cried off.'

'Do not waste too much time with Lord Arthur,' said Miss Chubb anxiously. 'He is engaged, or had you forgot?'

'I am not interested in him. He is too old and sophisticated and makes me feel uncomfortable. I have not told you, my dear Miss Chubb, but I have decided I do not wish to be married *at all*!'

Miss Chubb looked bewildered. 'Then, what is all this agony about? All our preparations, not to mention the horrendous expense of that rout?'

'Well, I thought, you know, that after a few

weeks of the Season, we should both retire somewhere in the country and be quiet and comfortable. But it would be pleasant to have a little fun first.'

'Fun?' echoed Miss Chubb in a hollow voice. She remembered her own stark terror when the Prince Regent had been announced, the worry and fret over the preparations, the skeleton of exposure as an impostor always standing in the closet waiting to leap out.

'Yes, *fun*,' said Felicity firmly. 'Now let us finish dressing, or we shall be late. It is nearly three o'clock already.'

But at three o'clock exactly, she and Miss Chubb descended the stairs just as Lord Arthur and Dolph arrived.

Felicity was wearing a blue muslin gown embroidered with little sprays of golden corn under a pelisse of gold silk. The Channing pearls glowed around her neck, and her jaunty straw hat was worn at a rakish angle on her red curls.

Miss Chubb, hoping to make up for Felicity's lack of display, was wearing a black velvet gown on which blazed an indeterminate number of jeweled brooches and pins. She was wearing a black velvet slouch hat that made her look like a highwayman.

She looked so worried and gloomy that Dolph, surveying the acres of black velvet, asked her whether she was in mourning.

'No, I am not,' said Miss Chubb sharply,

'and do not make personal remarks, young man.' Dolph was crushed into silence. He bowed his way out of the house backward toward the carriage, tripped on the top step, and somersaulted onto the pavement. Spinks, the butler, picked him up, and said gloomily, 'Pride goeth before destruction, and a haughty spirit before a fall.'

'Where on earth did you find such a biblical butler, Princess Felicity?' asked Lord Arthur as he drove off.

'I hired him in London,' said Felicity, and added primly, 'I am fortunate in having such a God-fearing staff.'

'What is the religion of Brasnia?'

Miss Chubb surveyed Lord Arthur with dislike. 'Orthodox Brasnian,' she said repressively.

'Oh, don't let's talk about Brasnia,' said Felicity hurriedly, 'or you will quite spoil my day. My poor country. So much turmoil. So many revolutions.'

Miss Chubb emitted something that sounded suspiciously like a groan.

'By George,' said Dolph. 'Got the Jacobites over there as well?'

'You were not listening, Dolph,' came Lord Arthur's amused voice. 'Princess Felicity does not want to talk about Brasnia!'

*   *   *

While Felicity was on her way to the balloon ascension, a portly gentleman called Mr. Guy Clough, a Virginian tobacco planter, was landing at Bristol. After a decent bottle of port at a good inn, he began to feel much recovered from the rigors of the voyage. He fished in his pocket and drew out a small oilskin packet and looked at it thoughtfully. A minister, the Reverend Hereward Harrington, had given him the packet before he sailed and had told him the strange story of the repentant kitchen maid, Bessie Redhill. Mr. Clough debated riding over to this Tregarthan Castle and confronting this Mr. Palfrey with the evidence of his crime. But a man who could half kill a servant and have her transported might not hesitate to shoot any bringer of bad news. Also in his capacious pockets, Mr. Clough carried several letters of introduction to people in court circles. The Prince Regent was also Prince of Wales and Duke of Cornwall. Tregarthan Castle was in Cornwall. Then it would be better to get word to the Prince of the evil that had taken place in his duchy and let him cope with it. Mr. Clough was a lazy man and preferred to put any action off to the last minute. He returned the will to his pocket and proceeded to forget about the whole thing.

* * *

And, also on that afternoon Mr. Palfrey was arriving in London. Life had been too uncomfortable of late, hounded as he was by the locals and reviled by the servants. He had decided to take himself off to London. Time was a great healer. He would visit the opera, see some plays, and generally enjoy himself. By the time he returned to Cornwall, he was sure the whole business would have died down.

*   *   *

The Belvedere Tea Gardens were crowded to overflowing. Felicity was glad of the crowd and the noise. Lord Arthur had talked generally about ballooning, plays, operas, and the balls to be held during the Season. He had not mentioned Brasnia. But there was a feeling of waiting about him, and every time his eyes fell on Felicity, they lit up with amusement.

When they had set out, the weather had been fine. But now a thin veil of clouds was covering the sun and a chill wind had sprung up. Lord Arthur solicitously produced bearskin carriage rugs for the ladies.

The great balloon had been already filled before their arrival, and its huge red-and-yellow-striped shape rose well above the crowd. The pilot balloon was sent off, then two carrier pigeons. The crowd, who had become bored with the long wait—for it had taken over two hours to inflate the balloon—cheered the pilot balloon and the pigeons wildly, glad to see some action at last.

Another cheer went up as the balloonist, a Mr. Peter Green, was escorted through the crowd. And another cheer rose as the cords were cut away and the gas-filled balloon began to rise.

Felicity's eyes filled with tears as she watched it. Lord Arthur's overwhelming masculine presence was making her extremely uncomfortable. She felt she would like to float away, like Mr. Green, far away from the troubles and worries of her masquerade, far up into the clouds, far away from staring, curious eyes. Lord Arthur silently handed her his handkerchief, and she stifled a sob and blew her nose. Silence fell on the crowd as the balloon began to climb and climb. When sand fell down from it like white smoke, the wind caught it, and it began to bear away steadily to the east. Felicity, like the crowd, watched and watched until the balloon grew smaller and smaller in the distance, until it finally disappeared into a bank of cloud.

And then all chaos broke loose. A crowd of people had been sitting on the wall of a house that bordered the tea gardens. As they swayed and shuffled to get down, the wall broke. There were terrific screams, and the crowd went mad. They pushed this way and that against the carriages. Lord Arthur's light curricle tilted wildly. Miss Chubb was thrown

133

out, and Dolph leapt down after her to try to rescue her from the stampeding crowd.

Lord Arthur's groom was holding the horses' reins and brandishing his whip as he tried to keep the crowd clear of the terrified horses.

'We're going to be crushed with the carriage,' cried Lord Arthur. He jumped down and lifted Felicity into his arms and began to force a way through the crowd, booting, kicking, and cursing as he cleared a path. He looked back over his shoulder. His groom had cut the horses free and was leading them safely away—just in time, for the curricle had been upended.

'Nearly safe,' said Lord Arthur in Felicity's ear. His arms were tightly around her, and above one hand he could feel the swell of her bosom. Her light body seemed a throbbing, pulsating thing. The effect of holding her so close was making his head swim. He looked down at her. She had her arms tightly around his neck, but her eyes were downcast.

He carried her clear of the crowd and stood for a moment, filled with an overwhelming reluctance to free her.

'Look at me, my princess,' he said softly. Felicity turned bewildered eyes up to his face and saw a light burning in those black eyes that made her tremble. He suddenly held her very tightly against him, smelling the light scent she wore, and feeling the trembling of her body.

Then he set her down, and, turning a little away from her, he said in a rough voice, 'There is a posting house quite near here. If you can walk that far, I shall hire some sort of carriage to take you home. You had better hold my hand. There are a great many unsavory people about.'

It would be all right to hold her hand, he thought. Any man, holding a beautiful young girl in his arms would have felt the way he did. But mere hand-holding was safe enough. He took her hand without looking at her. But a burning sensation seemed to run up his arm.

By the time they had reached the inn, he realized he wanted Felicity more than he had wanted any woman in the whole of his life. And he was engaged to be married.

'You are holding my hand very tightly,' said Felicity in a small voice, 'and we are well clear of the crowd.'

He released her hand. He had meant to ask for a private parlor so that she might be able to have some refreshment before he escorted her home. But he knew he could no longer be alone with her without wanting to touch her.

In a loud voice, he demanded a carriage, any carriage, brushed aside the landlord's apologies that there was only a gig, said he would take it, and drove Felicity home, only breaking his silence once to assure her that Dolph could be trusted to protect her companion.

She was in such a nervous turmoil that she should have been glad to see him go, but when he swept off his hat and bent over her hand to kiss it, she found herself saying, 'Shall we meet again?'

'Alas, I do not think so,' he said. 'I shall return to the country within the next few days.' He half turned away and then swung round again. 'But should you need any assistance, ma'am, tell Dolph, and he will know where to find me.'

Felicity trailed into the house and stood for a moment in the hall, dwarfed by all the rented magnificence of tiled floor, soaring double staircase, and oil paintings in heavy gilt frames.

Mr. Silver, a book in his hand, came out of the library at the far corner of the hall.

'Good afternoon, ma'am,' he said formally. Mr. Silver, like the rest of Felicity's employees, was well aware she was not a princess but always addressed her as if she were royal.

'Oh, Mr. Silver,' cried Felicity. 'Is Madame Chubiski returned?'

'Not as far as I know.'

'She was with me at the balloon ascension when a wall collapsed. There was rioting, and we became separated. Lord Arthur's friend, Mr. Godolphin, was with her.'

'Would you like me to go to Pentonville to look for her?' asked Mr. Silver anxiously.

'No, I am sure she is unharmed. But join me in the drawing room for some tea, and tell me how John Tremayne's education progresses.'

They drank tea and Mr. Silver reported that John was progressing favorably, but both strained their ears for a sound of the return of Miss Chubb. When a footman came in to light candles, Mr. Silver rose to his feet. 'With your permission, ma'am,' he said, 'I would like to go to Pentonville. I cannot feel easy in my mind. Madame Chubiski is rather shy and unused to London.'

'Shy? Unused to London, perhaps, but I would hardly call Madame Chub . . . iski *shy*.'

'I can assure you she is too gently bred a lady to be wandering about with a young boy of whom we know very little.'

'Then, by all means go,' cried Felicity.

Evening settled down over London. The parish lamps in the street outside were lit, and still Miss Chubb did not return.

At last Felicity heard the sound of a carriage stopping outside the house and ran out onto the front steps. But it was only Mr. Silver returning alone.

'I found no trace of her, ma'am,' he said, his lined face anxious. 'There were two people killed when that wall collapsed, and many more were injured in the rioting.'

'Oh, what shall I do?' cried Felicity. 'I cannot just wait here any longer, doing nothing. I know . . .'

She ran into the house and called for Spinks.

'Tell me,' she said to the butler, 'do you know the address of Lord Arthur Bessamy?'

'Yes, ma'am. When you told me to invite him to your rout, I made it my business to find out,' said Spinks. 'Lord Arthur lives in Curzon Street at Number 137.'

'That is only around the corner,' said Felicity, going into the drawing room and picking up her hat. Mr. Silver followed her in.

'You cannot go to Lord Arthur's house,' he said severely. 'That will not do at all.'

'Abstain from fleshy lusts, which war against the soul,' intoned the butler from the doorway, making them both jump.

'Oh, *Spinks*!' said Felicity crossly. 'Do behave yourself. I am only going to call on Lord Arthur to enlist his help in finding Madame Chubiski.'

'Then, I shall go,' said Mr. Silver quickly. 'For you to call at a gentleman's town house for any reason at all is just not done.'

Mr. Silver departed quickly, and once more Felicity was left to wait.

In ten minutes' time the tutor returned with Lord Arthur. 'You are fortunate, Princess,' said Lord Arthur. 'I was just leaving for my club when I received your message. I am sure you have nothing to worry about. Dolph is much more competent than he looks.'

'But you do not understand,' wailed Felicity. 'This is not like my companion at all. She may have been struck on the head; she may have

138

been abducted. Dear God, she was simply covered in jewels . . .'

Lord Arthur studied her distressed face and then said gently, 'I see you would feel better if you took some action. Your carriage is outside. Would you like to go back to the Belvedere Tea Gardens yourself and make inquiries? I am prepared to accompany you.'

'Thank you,' said Felicity.

'Then, I shall accompany you as well,' said the tutor firmly. 'You cannot go off alone with milord in a closed carriage.'

Lord Arthur nodded, and the three went out into the carriage and set off again in the direction of Pentonville.

'Tell me, Mr. Silver,' said Lord Arthur, 'when you were making inquiries for Madame Chubiski, how did you describe her?'

In the light of the carriage lamps, Mr. Silver's scholarly face registered surprise. 'Why, my lord, I gave a fair description. I asked if anyone had seen a handsome woman of regal bearing dressed in black velvet.'

Felicity felt she could sense Lord Arthur's amusement. What was there in Mr. Silver's innocent description that he could possibly find funny?

They traveled the rest of the way to Pentonville in silence. When they arrived at the tea gardens, Lord Arthur put a restraining hand on Mr. Silver's sleeve. 'Let me try by myself,' he said. 'You have already tried. I might have more success.'

Before the tutor could protest, Lord Arthur swung open the carriage door, stepped down, and strolled into the tea gardens. Waiters were still clearing up the mess left by the crowd. He went up to the nearest one and said, 'Hey, fellow, I am looking for a missing lady.'

'Better have a good description,' said the waiter sulkily, 'All the world and his wife were here today.'

Lord Arthur held up a guinea. 'Now, think,' he commanded, 'and this guinea will be for you. I seek a squat, somewhat elderly lady wearing a slouch hat like a highwayman, dressed in black velvet, and covered in jeweled brooches and pins. She is accompanied by a tubby, cheerful man.'

'Oh, them,' said the waiter.

'You know them?'

'I seen 'em with me own eyes,' said the waiter gleefully, reaching for the coin. 'I was over at The Black Dog—over there—for a pint of shrub, and there they were, singing their heads off.'

'And when was that?'

' 'Bout ten minutes ago.'

Lord Arthur returned to the carriage. 'I gather Dolph and Madame Chubiski are in the pub.'

He turned and walked off in the direction of The Black Dog. Felicity and Mr. Silver scrambled out of the carriage and ran after him. They caught up with Lord Arthur just as he opened the door of the tap.

Felicity peered over his arm and let out a gasp. Miss Chubb was standing on a table in the middle of the room, belting out the third verse of 'The Gay Hussar.' She had a tankard in her hand and was being accompanied on the fiddle by a ragged Highlander. Dolph was sitting down at the table on which she was standing, looking up at her with rapt attention.

'Disgraceful!' cried Mr. Silver.

'Wait!' commanded Lord Arthur.

Miss Chubb finished her song to wild cheers and shouts and was helped down from the table by Dolph, who gave her a smacking kiss on the cheek.

'Well, Dolph,' said Lord Arthur, strolling forward. 'Having fun?'

'Oh, the bestest ever,' said Dolph, peering at them blearily. 'Let's have another chorus. Oh, with a tow, row, tow, row . . .'

'Silence!' roared Mr. Silver. 'What have you done to this respectable lady, you . . . you rake? You have debased her. You have made a spectacle of her. By God, you shall answer me.'

'I . . . I . . . I,' babbled Dolph, goggling at the enraged tutor.

'No one is going to call anyone out,' said Lord Arthur soothingly. 'All outside. All home. Come along, Madame Chubiski. Your mistress has been very worried about you.'

'Don't w-want to go home,' hiccupped Miss

141

Chubb. 'Less have 'nother song.'

'We'll sing all you want,' said Felicity gently, 'when we get home—you, me, and Mr. Silver. Come along; there's a dear.'

Miss Chubb allowed herself to be led out, grumbling under her breath, 'You said I was to have fun. Said everybody mush have fun.'

'Yes, yes,' said Felicity, throwing Lord Arthur an anguished look. What if the drunken Miss Chubb forgot she was companion to a princess?

But as soon as the carriage moved off, both Miss Chubb and Dolph fell asleep, both snoring loudly, their heads rolling to the motion of the carriage. Felicity had Miss Chubb's full weight pressed against her, which in turn forced her to press against Lord Arthur. He smiled down at her and slid an arm about her shoulders. 'There, have you more room now?' he asked, as his pulse leapt at the feel of her body.

'Yes,' whispered Felicity dizzily.

Mr. Silver snorted, folded his arms, and glared grimly out the window.

As the carriage rattled through Berkeley Square, Lord Arthur found himself saying, 'I have decided to stay a little longer in town. Would you care to come driving with me—say on Friday—in three days' time? I shall call for you at five.'

He was not only a danger to this masquerade of hers, thought Felicity, he was a danger to her body, which seemed to be fusing hotly against the side of his own. When he smiled down into her eyes in that lazy, caressing way, as he was doing at that moment, he was a danger to her very soul. She must tell him she would never see him again. She must . . .

'Yes,' said Felicity weakly. 'I should like that very much.'

It took the efforts of three strong footmen to carry Miss Chubb upstairs to her bedchamber and four maids to undress her and put her to bed.

Felicity sat by the bed and held her unconscious companion's hand and looked down at her face. 'Oh, Miss Chubb,' she whispered. 'Why am I so very happy when it can all lead to disaster?'

*   *   *

Two days later Miss Barchester slowly lowered a copy of the *Morning Post.* It was a day old but carried a long description of the balloon ascension. The deaths of two people and the injuries of many only rated a small piece tagged on at the end. But the paragraph that riveted her attention went: THE ASCENSION WAS GRACED BY THE PRESENCE OF THE DIVINELY FAIR PRINCESS FELICITY OF BRASNIA. LORD ARTHUR BESSAMY IS THE ENVY OF ALL MEN, AS IT WAS HE WHO HAD

THE HONOR TO RESCUE HIS FAIR COMPANION FROM THE VULGAR AND RIOTING POPULACE, BEARING HER BOLDLY FROM THE SCENE IN HIS ARMS.

'Papa,' said Miss Barchester. 'Would it not be splendid to travel to London this weekend? Poor Lord Arthur must be pining away without me.'

'Don't like London,' grumbled Mr. Barchester. 'And if Lord Arthur is pining that bad, he's only got to come home.'

'Papa,' said Miss Barchester, a steely note in her voice. 'I have said I wish to go to London.'

'Eh, what? Oh, very well, m'dear,' sighed Mr. Barchester, who had long ago given up arguing with his strong-willed daughter.

CHAPTER EIGHT

It was the fashionable hour in Hyde Park. Spanking carriages darted along in the hazy spring sunlight. Dust rose from under hundreds of painted wheels. A carriage, particularly a lady's carriage, was not so much a means of transport as a sort of moving platform for the display of wealth. The more expensive the horses and carriage, the less used. No first-rate carriage horse was expected to travel more than fourteen miles a day at a maximum speed of ten miles per hour. In the

144

wealthiest establishments, a large, expensive retinue of coachmen, grooms, and stable boys was maintained so that milady or milord could drive out in grand style for one and a half hours a day, six days a week. Some of the ladies, beautifully attired in the most expensive fashions of the day, drove themselves with a liveried groom sitting on the rumble seat behind, or, occasionally, following on horseback at a distance that was great enough to appear respectful but not so great that he could not afford immediate assistance with horse or carriage in an emergency.

All of the servants were dressed in colorful livery with gay vertically-striped waistcoats, though the footmen wore horizontal stripes indoors. Their coats were ornamented with silver or gilt livery buttons. The stable staff wore highly polished top boots, while the footmen wore white silk stockings that were usually padded out with false calves if their legs were thin. The coats of arms on the carriages were miniature works of art, and the whole display had an air of idle opulence.

But underneath all this atmosphere of languid elegance, each member of society was in deadly earnest. Mamas studied the faces of the eligibles for signs of interest while their daughters giggled and fluttered, and used fans and eyes to the best effect. Parvenus cut their country relatives dead as they fawned on the notables.

And Lord Arthur Bessamy was discovering, to his amazement, that one could make love to a lady with one's whole body without touching her or moving an inch. His eyes caressed the smooth pearl of her cheeks, his arms, correctly holding his cane and his gloves, were, in his mind's eye, clasped tightly about the slimness of her waist. His lips burned against hers in his imagination.

Felicity sensed a wave of sensuality emanating from him without quite knowing what it was, without knowing why her whole body seemed drawn to him, why her lips felt hot and swollen, and her breasts strained against the thinness of demure muslin.

Dolph was in good spirits, cheerfully waving to everyone he knew. Miss Chubb was downcast, her eyes red. Felicity had overheard Miss Chubb having the most terrible row with the tutor, but when asked about it, Miss Chubb had only sniveled dismally and refused to explain.

Felicity grew more uncomfortably aware of her own reddening cheeks and treacherously throbbing body. Lord Arthur was engaged to be married, she told herself firmly, and then wondered why that thought made her feel so depressed. When they stopped as a carriage full of Lord Arthur's relatives pulled up beside them, Felicity was glad of their company, glad to have Lord Arthur's disturbing attention taken away from her. But her peace of mind did not last long. One faded aunt with a long, drooping nose and pale, inquisitive eyes, said, 'Bessamy, you have forgot your manners. Introduce us immediately to Miss Barchester—or do you mean to keep her away from us until the wedding?'

'This is not Miss Barchester,' said Lord Arthur equably. 'Allow me to present Princess Felicity of Brasnia.' He then introduced his relatives to his party. Two aunts, two uncles, and two small female cousins bowed to Felicity and stared at her in open curiosity. 'Charmed,' said the inquisitive aunt who had been introduced as Mrs. Chester-Vyne. 'Do you mean to reside in London for long, Your Highness?'

'Only for a few weeks of the Season, Mrs. Chester-Vyne.'

'I am very good at geography and have a knowledge of the globes,' piped up a small cousin with a face like a ferret. 'I have never heard of Brasnia.'

'Nor I,' said Mr. Chester-Vyne, who looked remarkably like his long-nosed wife.

'Dear me,' said Lord Arthur. 'Never heard of Brasnia? I am ashamed of you all. It is quite lovely this time of year. They have the Festival of Manhood about now. All the young men in the villages are stripped quite naked and lashed . . .'

'Here, now!' protested Mr. Chester-Vyne. 'Ladies present.'

'*Stripped naked and lashed,*' went on Lord Arthur firmly, 'until the blood runs. They are then sponged clean by the village maidens who are bare to the waist. A most touching ceremony, and quite colorful.'

'Bessamy!' said Mrs. Chester-Vyne awfully. 'We have no wish to have our sensibilities bruised by macabre tales of a barbaric race. Walk on, John.'

The coachman raised his whip, and the relatives drove off with many a backward offended glance.

'By Jove!' said Dolph. 'You have found out a lot about Brasnia.'

'Not I,' said Lord Arthur cheerfully. 'I merely wanted to be shot of them. You must tell me the truth about Brasnia someday, Princess.'

'Yes, I must, mustn't I,' said Felicity in a small voice. She took little consolation from the fact that the encounter with Lord Arthur's relatives had had the same effect as a bucket of cold water being poured over her.

'Going to the opera tonight?' she realized Dolph was asking.

'We have no plans for this evening,' said Felicity.

'Then, you must come with us!' cried Dolph. 'Lord Arthur has a box, and you would be delighted to take the ladies along, now wouldn't you, Arthur?'

A vision of his fiancée's pale, cold face rose

before Lord Arthur's eyes.

'You simply must come,' he said. 'Catalini is singing. We shall call for you at eight.'

'I don't think I should attend,' sniffed Miss Chubb. 'I know Mr. Silver will be quite furious with me.'

Felicity looked at her in surprise. 'What on earth has our tutor to do with where we go?'

'Mr. Silver,' said Miss Chubb heavily, 'thinks I behaved in a most unladylike way after the balloon ascension.'

'Then, I suggest you put Mr. Silver firmly in his place,' said Dolph.

'Then, you will come?' asked Lord Arthur, saying to himself, just one more evening and then I shall behave myself.

Just one more time, thought Felicity.

'Yes,' she said. 'And do not look so worried, Madame Chubiski. I shall talk to Mr. Silver most sternly if he makes any trouble.'

*   *   *

Mr. Palfrey was sitting at the toilet table in a room in Limmer's in Conduit Street, arranging his hair with the curling tongs, when a hotel servant arrived to say he had managed to secure Mr. Palfrey a seat in the pit at the opera.

Mr. Palfrey tipped him generously. His heart lifted. He was glad he had come to London. It was wonderful to be away from accusing Cornish eyes. Let the fuss die down, and then he could return to his search for the jewels. Somewhere at the bottom of the ocean, flashing fire in the green depths, lay the Channing diamonds. He had studied them minutely in that portrait at the castle until he felt he knew every stone.

As usual, he fussed a great deal over his appearance. Then he realized his cumbersome traveling coach was not suitable for a short journey, and besides, it was round in the mews and would take an age for the horses to be harnessed up. He debated whether to walk, but fear of arriving at the opera with muddied heels and possibly dirty stockings made him ring the bell and request a hack.

It was nine o'clock before Mr. Palfrey reached the opera house. The seats in the pit were simply long wooden benches, and they were already packed to capacity by lounging bucks and bloods by the time he arrived. He retreated from the pit and tipped an usher, who told him that a certain Sir Jeffrey Dawes would not be using his box that evening, and Mr. Palfrey would be able to use it.

Comfortably ensconced in a side box, Mr. Palfrey immediately raised his glass to his eye and scanned the house. He let out a slow breath of pleasure. This was where he belonged, not hidden away in some castle in Cornwall. Fans fluttered and jewels glittered on men and women alike.

His eye, magnified by the glass, traveled along the row of boxes opposite—and then he let it drop with a squawk and turned quite white under his paint.

'Shhh,' hissed a dowager venomously from the box next to his.

Mr. Palfrey sat trembling. Surely that had been Felicity Channing in the box opposite!

Catalini's lovely voice soared and fell. She had the power to make all these society members look at her and listen to her—a rare feat, as most attended the opera because it was fashionable to do so and were usually not in the slightest interested in what was taking place on the stage.

Mr. Palfrey took a deep breath and raised his glass again.

It *was* Felicity! And a Felicity blazing and flashing with diamonds, the Channing diamonds that he had come to know so well from studying that portrait at Tregarthan Castle.

Now he shook with rage. Just wait until those servants and yokels in Cornwall heard about this!

He could barely contain himself until the opera was over. Two people had left Felicity's box, but she was still there herself with a male companion. Mr. Palfrey did not recognize Lord Arthur. What if they did not stay for the farce? It would be hard to reach them.

He rose to his feet and scurried along the

corridor behind the boxes, shaking off the clutching hands of the prostitutes.

In his rage and confusion, he opened the doors of several wrong boxes before he hit the right one.

'Well, Felicity Channing,' he said in a voice squeaky with outrage. 'And what have you to say for yourself?'

The little figure with her back to him remained absolutely still. The man beside Felicity rose to his feet. Now Mr. Palfrey recognized Lord Arthur.

'What the deuce do you mean by this outrage?' demanded Lord Arthur, towering over Mr. Palfrey. 'This lady is the Princess Felicity of Brasnia.'

'Princess, my foot!' screeched Mr. Palfrey. 'That's my stepdaughter, the minx. And those are my jewels.'

He made a move forward to grasp Felicity's shoulder and then gasped as Lord Arthur pushed him back.

'Leave immediately,' said Lord Arthur, 'or I shall call you out.'

"But that is my stepdaughter,' cried Mr. Palfrey. 'She pretended to die in order to trick me.'

'Your Royal Highness,' said Lord Arthur, 'before I throw this fellow downstairs, do you wish to take a look at him? Perhaps he is a former servant of yours whose mind has become deranged.'

'Servant!' shouted Mr. Palfrey. 'Do I look like a servant?'

Felicity stood up and turned about.

She looked coldly at Mr. Palfrey. 'I have never seen this man before in my life,' she said steadily.

Her eyes were cold, and her expression haughty. All in that moment, Mr. Palfrey began to fear he had made a terrible mistake. The diamonds on her head and at her throat blazed with such a light that he could no longer be sure they were the Channing jewels, for their prismatic fire nearly prevented him from seeing the individual stones. But it was the beauty of the girl in front of him that took him aback. For Mr. Palfrey had convinced himself that Felicity was plain. In his memory, she was a drab little thing with carroty hair, not a regal goddess like the lady facing him.

He became aware that everyone in the house had begun to stare at Lord Arthur's box. Lord Arthur looked on the point of suggesting a duel.

'Pray accept my apologies,' babbled Mr. Palfrey. 'The resemblance is astonishing. You remember me, do you not, Lord Arthur? You were there when my poor Felicity was found missing.'

Lord Arthur continued to regard him as if he were something that had crept out from under a stone, but Felicity spoke again, her voice strangely accented. 'No doubt,' she said, 'grief over the death of your stepdaughter has sadly turned your brain.' Then she sat down again with her back to him.

Stammering apologies, Mr. Palfrey bowed his way out.

'I have the headache,' said Felicity. 'I wish to go home.'

'First Madame Chubiski with a headache, and now you,' said Lord Arthur. 'Come along. You are looking very white. Did that silly little man upset you?'

'Yes. What is all this about his stepdaughter, my lord? And do you know him?' Felicity trembled as she waited for his reply. For if he had not known she was an impostor before, surely he knew now.

'I met him once,' said Lord Arthur in a bored voice. 'His stepdaughter, also called Felicity, was running away from him. She fell over a cliff in a storm.'

'How terrible!'

'Indeed, yes. I trust you do not have such dreadful happenings in Brasnia.'

Felicity wanted to cry out to him that she was sure he had not believed one word of her nonsense, but there was still a little element of doubt, still a little hope that he believed her. She did not know why it was, but she felt uneasy and breathless and uncomfortable with him, and wretchedly lonely and afraid the minute he went away.

In the carriage ride home, with Lord Arthur

riding on the box—for it was a closed carriage and she would have been compromised had he traveled inside with her—Felicity wondered desperately what to do. Thank goodness Miss Chubb had felt ill and had left with Dolph. Those two would surely have made up Mr. Palfrey's mind for him. She would need to leave London. She would need to get away, for she was sure that if Mr. Palfrey saw her with Miss Chubb, then the game would be up. And it would be folly to continue to see Lord Arthur. He was engaged to another woman.

To her dismay, Lord Arthur followed her into the house in Chesterfield Street.

She turned in the hall to tell him he must leave and then her eye fell on the enormous gold-crested card. She picked it up. It was an invitation to the Queen's drawing room in two weeks' time.

'The royal summons, eh?' said Lord Arthur, reading it over her shoulder.

'Do I have to go?' asked Felicity.

'It would certainly look most odd if you did not.'

Felicity thought rapidly. Two weeks. She would leave town in the morning and return just for the Queen's drawing room, and then Princess Felicity of Brasnia would disappear forever.

'Will you come driving with me tomorrow?' Lord Arthur asked.

'N-no,' said Felicity. 'I am unwell and need

country air. We shall be leaving in the morning.'

He went very still, and then he said lightly, 'And where are you bound?'

'I had not decided.'

'May I suggest Brighton? It is quite near London, and it is possible to find comfortable accommodation out of Season.'

'Perhaps. Perhaps that would be best.' Felicity held out her hand. 'Good-bye, Lord Arthur,' she said firmly. 'I doubt if we shall meet again.'

He took her hand in his and smiled down into her eyes. She looked up at him with a dazed, drowned look. He dropped her hand and then placed his own hands lightly on her shoulders. His mouth began to descend toward her own. He kissed her very lightly on the lips, and then raised his head and looked at her in a sort of wonder. His arms slid from her shoulders to settle at her waist, and then he jerked her tightly against him and kissed her again, and both went whirling off into a warm sensual blackness while the clock in the hall ticked away the seconds, and then the minutes, as his mouth moved languorously against her own and passion sang in his veins.

'Is that you, Felicity?' came Miss Chubb's voice. And then her heavy tread sounded in the corridor upstairs.

They broke apart, breathing heavily as if they had been running.

'You shouldn't have . . .' whispered Felicity.

'Brighton,' he said firmly. 'Go to Brighton.'

He turned on his heel, and then he was gone, leaving Felicity standing in the hall, her hand to her lips.

*   *   *

The council of war went on long into the night. John Tremayne was to ride ahead to Brighton and rent a house and then ride out to the first posting house on the road outside Brighton to give them the address. Felicity's dressmaker's dummy was to be sent to the dressmaker with the promise of double money if a court dress were made and ready in time for the Queen's drawing room.

'Brighton is certainly an excellent place to choose,' said Mr. Silver. 'What made you choose Brighton, ma'am?'

'Oh, I don't know,' said Felicity vaguely. For she was sure there would be protests if she said the suggestion had come from Lord Arthur. Mr. Silver considered Lord Arthur and his friend, Dolph, to be corrupt and evil men who encouraged ladies like Miss Chubiski to drink to excess, and Miss Chubb herself had become more and more worried about Felicity and Lord Arthur. Felicity had not told her about the embrace. Miss Chubb, she knew, would be deeply shocked.

Lord Arthur made ready to go out in search of Dolph the next day to see if that young man would fancy a trip to Brighton. But the fact that he was engaged to be married to Miss Martha Barchester was forcibly brought home to him when his footman handed him a letter. With a sinking heart, he recognized the seal. He crackled open the parchment. The letter was from Miss Barchester, saying that she and her parents were staying at the Crillon Hotel. Lord Arthur would no doubt be delighted and amazed to see her so soon. His presence was expected at the earliest moment.

He took a deep breath. He must disengage himself from Miss Barchester at the earliest opportunity. But what excuse did he have? That he had never been in love before? That he had never believed in such an emotion? That his heart was not in London, it was on the road to Brighton?

But did poor Miss Barchester deserve to be jilted because she no longer held any magic for him? That calmness and stillness of hers that had so attracted him now seemed dull. He felt like a cad.

He took himself off to the Crillon Hotel, preferring to walk, and so absorbed in his worries that he did not notice he was being followed.

Mr. Palfrey had had a quite dreadful night.

He had dreamed of Felicity, and on waking, the dream face and the face of Princess Felicity merged in his mind and became one. He had to see her again, just to make sure. By diligently questioning the hotel staff, he obtained the princess's address in Chesterfield Gardens and set out there at eleven in the morning while the streets of the West End were still quiet. But after half an hour of surveying the house from the opposite side of the street, he had an uneasy feeling there was no one at home.

At last, summoning up his courage, he crossed over and hammered on the knocker. He could hear the sound of his knocking echoing away into emptiness inside. A butler came out of the house next door and stood on the step and looked up and down the street.

'Tell me, my good man,' called Mr. Palfrey, 'is the princess in residence?'

'Her Royal Highness and all her staff left early this morning,' said the butler.

Mr. Palfrey stood, baffled. He had been all set to take some sort of action to ease his mind. There must be something he could do.

'Do you know where they have gone?' he asked.

The butler shook his powdered wig.

Mr. Palfrey paced restlessly up and down. Then his face cleared. She had been with Lord Arthur Bessamy. If he could find Lord Arthur, then that gentleman might lead him to the whereabouts of the mysterious princess. 'Do you know where a certain Lord Arthur Bessamy resides?' he asked.

The butler turned his head away in disdain. Mr. Palfrey took two gold sovereigns out of his pocket and clinked them in his hands. The butler's head jerked round. 'Just around the corner, sir,' he said with an ingratiating smile. 'Number 137.'

'Thank you, fellow,' said Mr. Palfrey cockily and, returning the sovereigns to his pocket, strolled off down the street and then flinched as a lump of dried horse manure flew past his ear and the outraged butler's screech of 'Skinflint!' followed him around the corner into Curzon Street.

Then he stopped. Lord Arthur was emerging from his house. He was too formidable a man to be approached. Mr. Palfrey set out to follow.

He had to scurry to keep up with Lord Arthur's long legs. Soon he saw his quarry walking into the Crillon Hotel. He followed at a discreet distance, saw the hotel manager bowing and scraping, and then saw Lord Arthur mounting the stairs.

He waited a few moments and then strolled into the hotel and approached the manager. 'I am desirous to know who it is Lord Arthur is meeting,' he said, holding out the two sovereigns he had failed to give to the butler. The manager took the money, put it in the pocket of his tails, dabbed his mouth fastidiously with a handkerchief, and said, 'Get out. We do not discuss anything to do with our guests or noble visitors.'

'Then, give me my money back this instant.'

'What money?' said the manager. 'Here! Jeremy, Peter, throw this fellow out.'

Mr. Palfrey cast a scared look at the approaching waiters and ran out into the street. He stood for a moment and then crossed the road and skulked in a doorway.

*   *   *

When Lord Arthur entered the Barchesters' hotel drawing room, he was relieved to see only Mr. Barchester. He did not yet feel ready to face his soon-to-be disengaged fiancée.

'Martha's putting on her pretties,' said Mr. Barchester. 'Sit down, sit down, Bessamy. Help yourself to wine.'

Lord Arthur poured himself a glass of burgundy and sat down opposite Mr. Barchester. 'I fear you will not be pleased to see me when you learn the reason for my visit.'

Mr. Barchester's shrewd little eyes twinkled in the pads of fat that were his cheeks. 'I'll try to bear up,' he said. 'What's to do?'

'What would you say, sir, were I to tell you that I have fallen in love for the first time in my life, and, alas, not with your daughter?'

There was a long silence. Then Mr.

Barchester tilted his glass of port to his mouth and took a gulp. 'That's better,' he said. 'Oh, well, as to your question, I would say I have been planning new stables this past age.'

Lord Arthur looked in amazement at Mr. Barchester. One of Mr. Barchester's fat eyelids drooped in a wink. 'Come on, Bessamy,' he said. 'You always struck me as being a knowing cove.'

'So,' said Lord Arthur slowly, 'am I to take it that if I build new stables for you, the Barchester family will not sue me for breach of promise?'

'That's right,' said Mr. Barchester cheerfully.

'You do not seem in the least surprised. I feel a cad and a charlatan for treating your daughter so.'

'She's used to it,' said Mr. Barchester heartlessly. 'See that new wing at Hapsmere Manor? That was when Sir Henry Carruthers cried off. And the fine tiled roof? That was . . . let me see . . . ah, that was Mr. Tommy Bradshaw. The staircase was the Honorable Peter Chambers, but then he didn't have too much of the ready . . .'

'How many times has Miss Barchester been engaged?'

''Bout four or five. M'wife'll put you straight.'

'But don't you see,' said Lord Arthur, appalled, 'I cannot possibly bring myself to break the engagement now! After all these disappointments . . . I would feel like a monster.'

'Take Martha out for a little walk and have a talk to her,' said Mr. Barchester. 'Martha's little talks always do the trick. You'll be back here like a rat up a spout, begging to give me those new stables.'

Lord Arthur was not able to say any more, for at that moment the door opened and Miss Barchester walked in, accompanied by her mother. She was wearing a severe walking dress of old-fashioned cut and a poke bonnet. She treated Lord Arthur to a cool smile.

'Off you go, Martha,' said her father heartily. 'Bessamy here's come to take you for a little walk.'

As they made their way to Hyde Park, Lord Arthur had an odd feeling he was being followed. He turned around sharply several times, but the streets were very busy and no one appeared to be paying him any particular interest.

Martha was talking steadily in a level voice and at last he was able to take in what she was saying.

'When we are married, I should like to spend most of the year in town,' said Miss Barchester. 'The ladies' fashions are sadly skimpy, and fashion would have a new leader.'

'In yourself?' asked Lord Arthur, glancing down at her walking dress and wondering how she had managed to find material that was so drab, so mud-colored.

'Of course! And I am sure you will agree with me that marriages in which men spend all their time at their clubs end in disaster.'

'On the contrary, it might be the saving of many.'

'You are funning, of course. I have not told you before, Lord Arthur, but there is a certain levity about you which must be curbed.'

Lord Arthur stopped listening to her, saving all his energies for the scene he knew must surely break about his head when he told her he no longer wished to marry her.

How could he have ever for a moment thought she might make a suitable wife? Well, she had seemed so calm, so docile, so biddable.

He led her to an iron bench by the Serpentine and dusted it before they sat down. There was a crackling and a rustling in the bushes behind him, and Miss Barchester looked around nervously.

'Probably a dog,' said Lord Arthur.

Mr. Palfrey scrunched down in the bushes and strained his ears.

In a flat voice, Lord Arthur proceeded to tell Miss Barchester that he wished to terminate their engagement.

She heard him in silence and then said, 'You will soon come to your senses. In any case, I refuse to release you.'

'Even when you know this marriage would now make me unhappy?'

'Although you are not a young man,' said Miss Barchester coyly, 'I fear the company of a certain princess has turned your head. Now, do be sensible. I am sure you do not want a scandal. Gentlemen are like little boys. They never seem to know their own minds—which is why we ladies must make the decisions for them. Don't be silly, Lord Arthur. We are going to be married, and you have nothing to say in the matter.'

'Madam! You have just persuaded me to go to any lengths to be free of you. Come, I shall escort you back to your parents.'

'I prefer to stay here. It is pleasant.'

'Then, stay by yourself,' said Lord Arthur wrathfully, and, getting to his feet, he strode off.

He went straight back to the Crillon, up the stairs, and into the drawing room.

Mr. Barchester rubbed his chubby hands when he saw his face. 'Have some more wine, dear boy!' he cried. 'And let us discuss the new stables.'

*   *   *

Miss Barchester screamed as a dandified, middle-aged man crashed out of the bushes behind her.

'Hush, dear lady,' he said. 'I am here to help

165

you. Lord Arthur Bessamy was at the opera t'other night with a young lady calling herself Princess Felicity of Brasnia.'

The scream for help died stillborn on Miss Barchester's thin lips.

'Who are you?' she demanded sharply.

Mr. Palfrey came around and sat down beside her. 'Let me explain . . .' he began.

CHAPTER NINE

'Do you know,' said Dolph, as he and Lord Arthur bowled along the Brighton Road, 'I met an old tutor of mine from Oxford. Asked him about Brasnia and he said he had never heard of it.'

'Odd, the ignorance of some of those Oxford dons,' said Lord Arthur. 'Come to think of it, it's quite disgraceful.'

'But he's a clever chap. Everybody says so. Now, you tell me. Where's Brasnia?'

'It is up near the Arctic Circle,' said Lord Arthur. 'Quite a small country, very savage, full of polar bears and . . .'

'What kind of bears?'

'White. All over. So that they can hide themselves in the snow. As I was saying before I was so rudely interrupted, the inhabitants live in mansions carved out of ice in the winter, and, in the summer they live in tents made out of reindeer skin.'

'But don't they have cities . . . towns? I mean doesn't the princess have a castle?'

'Of course she does. A white castle with long, glittering icicles hanging from the towers. It was built in the thirteenth century by Georgi the Horrible. He kept four maidens locked up at one time, which is why the castle has four tall towers. When he had . . . er . . . had his way with them, he fed them to his pet bears.'

'The white ones?' said Dolph suspiciously.

'Except when they fed on the maidens. Then they turned a delicate, rosy pink.'

'They must be very well-educated people. I mean, Miss Chubiski speaks English very well.'

'Yes, she does, doesn't she. Alas, it is only the aristocracy who can enjoy the benefits of education. There is no middle class—only aristocracy and peasants. The peasants are illiterate to a man.'

'Look here, don't tell me the shopkeepers are all aristocrats. How do they keep the books?'

'They don't. The price of each article is indicated by so many stamps of the foot, rather like that educated pig at Bartholomew Fair.'

'What if something cost a hundred guineas? The shopkeeper would have a sore foot before he got the price out. And what about pounds, shillings, and pence?'

'My dear, dear Dolph, nothing so complicated. It is a very poor country, so they don't have anything at all that costs over the equivalent of one pound. They have only a small coin called a secrudo, made of tin.'

'Why do I get the feeling you're talking rubbish?' said Dolph. 'Go on. Tell me about the ruler.'

'The king is . . .'

'Now, wait a minute, you told Prinny that Brasnia was a principality.'

'So I did, and I made the whole thing up then. Now you are hearing the real truth. King Georgi the Fourth, is Princess Felicity's uncle. He poisoned his queen because he wanted to keep up the family tradition of incarcerating maidens in the four towers and subsequently feeding them to the bears. He . . . Dolph, this is all very interesting, and you keep twisting your head about.'

'Well, it's a funny thing, but I was getting a nasty, prickling feeling in the back of my neck. I thought it was because you were prosing on about maidens being fed to bears. But I turned about and took a glance down the road behind. There's a traveling carriage, and as I looked, a head popped out the window and the passenger yelled something to the driver. I only caught a glimpse, but it looked horribly like that Mr. Palfrey.'

'More than likely. I was unfortunate enough to meet him at the opera last night. We'll shake him loose. Long roundabout journey to Brighton, I am afraid.'

Lord Arthur turned off the Brighton road and drove some ten miles to where Lord Achesham, a friend of his father's, had a mansion. His lordship was not at home, but his butler was delighted to receive a hefty tip to show them the back way out of the estate, and then to tell anyone asking for them that they were guests of Lord Achesham and would be staying for some time. And if an impertinent fellow should inquire after a certain Princess Felicity, the butler was to say that she, too, was in residence. If he insisted on seeing the princess, he was to be shown out.

*   *   *

Felicity had told John Tremayne not to use her fake title when he rented a house. She had no wish to be brought to the attention of the worthies of Brighton. It had proved remarkably easy for John to find a suitable residence large enough for Felicity and her staff. Until the end of the Season, Brighton was a quiet place. In June, when the Prince arrived with his court and followers, it would spring into life.

It was wonderful to settle down into relative anonymity. She often thought of Lord Arthur, but distance from him had given her courage. A man who was engaged to one lady, and yet could kiss another, was not a gentleman.

A few callers had tried to leave cards with

Miss Chubb—Felicity having made the governess take the house in her name—as a certain interest had been provoked in the lady who had taken one of the largest houses in Brighton. But gloomy Spinks had told them all that Miss Chubb did not wish to see anyone. The advantage of renting a house complete with furniture and arriving with a highly trained staff meant Felicity had been able to settle in almost immediately.

No callers to Spinks also included Lord Arthur Bessamy and Mr. Charles Godolphin, who arrived on the doorstep three days after Felicity's arrival, it having taken them the whole of the previous day to track her down.

Lord Arthur, however, insisted on leaving his card, and that was to cause ructions. Felicity, determined to be good, might not have decided to see him had not both Miss Chubb and Mr. Silver cried out against the very idea. Now Mr. Silver, that assiduous reader of newspapers, could have told his young mistress that an announcement of the termination of Lord Arthur's engagement had just appeared in the *Times*. But it was not Lord Arthur he distrusted so much as Dolph, and so he deliberately did not tell her. Felicity herself rarely read the newspapers, finding the long tales of war in the Spanish peninsula frightening and depressing, and the social gossip a mixture of malice and trivia. But Miss Chubb and Mr. Silver's orders that she must not have anything more to do with Lord Arthur set up a spirit of perversity in Felicity. The memory of that kiss was achingly sweet. She was frightened at the idea of the approaching visit to the Queen's drawing room and craved the reassurance of Lord Arthur's presence.

Accordingly, when Lord Arthur and Dolph called the following day, Felicity had been watching for them and commanded Spinks to allow them to enter.

Lord Arthur promptly suggested that Felicity should accompany him on a drive, and Dolph, taking his cue, said he would be happy to stay and keep Miss Chubb company. Mr. Silver muttered something rude under his breath, and went out for a long walk.

The day was sparkling and brisk as Lord Arthur drove Felicity up over the downs. He laughed at her fears over her forthcoming presentation to the Queen. 'It is not a terrifying occasion,' he said. 'People push and shove to get into the drawing room. They bow or curtsey, as the case may be. Her Majesty takes snuff and looks bored. And then they shove and fight back downstairs, usually to find that their disposables, such as shawls, hats, tippets, and cloaks, have been stolen.'

'But surely there are some people who fall ill, who are unable to attend,' said Felicity. 'I could be one of them.'

'It would be considered very odd in a . . .

visiting royalty?'

His voice ended on a question, and Felicity blushed. 'Why are you in Brighton, my lord?' she asked, as he stopped his team on a grassy hill above the sea.

'Now, I should have thought that was obvious. I came in pursuit of you, my princess.'

Felicity turned her head away and fiddled with the long blue satin ribbons of her gown. 'My lord, I must remind you that you are engaged to Miss Barchester.'

'No longer. I disengaged myself.'

Felicity suddenly felt ridiculously happy. But his next words took all that happiness away. 'Now, Princess Felicity,' he said, 'do you not think it is time you told me all about Brasnia?'

She hung her head. She longed to tell him the truth, but would he believe her? I took the jewels and ran. But what proof had she that the jewels were really hers? And how could their relationship deepen unless she did tell him the truth?

'Don't look so miserable,' he said gently. 'We will have all our married life before us to talk about the wretched place.'

Felicity's wide eyes flew to meet his. 'You wish to marry me?'

'Of course. I do not kiss gently bred ladies unless my intentions are serious, and they have never before been as serious as this.'

'I cannot marry you,' said Felicity miserably. He jumped lightly down from the carriage and led his team of horses to a stunted tree and tethered them. Then he helped Felicity to alight.

'Now, why can't you marry me?' he said.

'My family would forbid it.'

'Ah, back to Brasnia again. Perhaps I should go there and ask whoever I need to ask.'

'That would not answer. I am already betrothed.'

'To whom?'

'Prince Ivan, my first cousin.'

'Here. You cannot go around marrying first cousins. You'll have a nursery full of imbeciles. My dearest, is it not time you told me the truth?'

Felicity walked a little ahead of him in silence.

'You see, you are going to marry me,' he said, catching up with her. 'And I then must go and see my family to tell them the good news, and then I must find a special license because I do not want to wait. Are you afraid of me?'

Felicity turned to face him. 'Oh, yes,' she whispered. 'Very afraid.'

He looked at her ruefully. 'I must do something to end this farce. I never thought to use force, but . . .'

He deftly kicked Felicity's legs from under her, and as she fell backward on the springy turf, he crouched down beside her and pinioned her arms above her head.

'Now,' he said, 'let's kiss some of that

Brasnian nonsense out of you.'

'You are stronger than I am,' said Felicity with pathetic dignity. 'I can only appeal to your honor, if you do have any.'

He smiled down at her wickedly. 'Not a scrap,' he said softly, and then his mouth descended on hers.

As he kissed her softly, he released her wrists, only to pull her body into his arms. Felicity planned to lie cold and unresisting in order to bring him to his senses. But her lips had a will of their own, and her body refused to listen to frantic messages from her brain and arched against his. As he felt her response he freed her mouth and kissed her neck. 'Brasnia,' he whispered against her skin. 'Come along now. Tell me about Brasnia or I shall forget myself and leave you with no choice but to marry me. Brasnia!'

'No!' said Felicity.

Her dress was high-waisted and stiffened, to push her breasts up against the low neckline. He kissed the top of each breast and then rolled on top of her, pressing her into the ground with the weight of his body and began caressing her mouth again with his lips, soft stroking kisses that were more devastating than any savage assault.

Felicity let out a sort of gurgling moan, and he raised his head. Her hat had tumbled off onto the grass, and her red hair had come free of its pins and lay in a fiery cloud about her face.

'Oh, I shall tell you,' she sighed, 'and then you will go away and forget about me.'

'I doubt it, Mr. Freddy Channing, Miss Felicity Channing and Your Royal Highness. I doubt it very much.'

'You knew,' said Felicity. 'You knew all along.'

'Of course I did, my widgeon! But I wanted you to trust me, to tell me. I hope I can recognize a pretty girl even when dressed in men's clothes. And I was there, you know, when Palfrey thought you had plunged to your death. It was when I fished a little girl's dress out of the sea that I realized you had only pretended to die. You might have left behind a more convincing wardrobe, you idiot.'

'I can't think with you lying on top of me in this disgraceful way,' said Felicity.

He rolled to one side, only to gather her in his arms again. 'Now, go on,' he said. 'Where did you get the money to buy all those jewels?'

'They are mine,' said Felicity. 'Mama left a codicil the day she died, but Mr. Palfrey did not mention it. I think he found it and burned it. I knew where the jewels were hidden. It was on the day after I had seen the baron that Miss Chubb and John Tremayne told me they had been hatching a plot. It seems outrageous now, dangerous and silly. But I had to escape.'

'So you had,' he said, smoothing her hair. 'So you will make a last grand appearance as the princess at the drawing room, and then we shall be married. The princess will disappear, and Miss Felicity Channing will take her place in time for the wedding.'

'But Mr. Palfrey . . . ?'

'Mr. Palfrey will do nothing to cross swords with me. As my wife, no one will be able to harm you.'

'Do you love me?'

Lord Arthur began to laugh. 'I break my engagement, I chase you to Brighton, I make love to you on this drafty hilltop, and I ask you to marry me. Of course I love you. I think I loved you from the moment I saw you in that silly disguise at The Green Dolphin.'

'Then, why did you become engaged to Miss Barchester?'

'I did not know then I loved you. I thought you a wild, ferocious little girl who had run away and would probably never be seen again.' He gave her a little shake. 'Do you love me, Felicity?'

'Yes.'

'Then, prove it. Kiss me!'

Felicity wound her arms about his neck and kissed him with all her heart. He kissed her back and kept on kissing her until the sun went down and a chill wind began to blow in from the sea.

*   *   *

Mr. Palfrey had been billeted at an inferior inn near Lord Achesham's house for a week. Every day he went out and walked up and down outside the main gates leading to the mansion, and every evening he returned feeling defeated. He had written to Miss Barchester to tell her of his lack of progress. She wrote back to say that the list of guests to attend the Queen's drawing room included the name of Princess Felicity of Brasnia. She herself was to attend, and if Mr. Palfrey had not been invited, he had only to bribe a certain chancellor, pointed out Mr. Barchester's daughter.

Reading this welcome letter over a dinner of stringy mutton and watery beans washed down with acid claret, Mr. Palfrey heaved a sigh of relief. All he had to do was to return to London and wait. Miss Barchester was a woman after his own heart. She had encouraged him that first day they had met by saying she was sure there was no such place as Brasnia and that poor Lord Arthur had been tricked by a scheming adventuress. Should that adventuress turn out to be Felicity Channing, then she would be unmasked in front of the Queen. Mr. Palfrey had quailed before the drama of this idea, suggesting a quieter exposure of the impostor, but Miss Barchester had overridden his protests.

Miss Barchester thirsted to take her place on the center stage of society, a place she felt had been snatched from her by Felicity. Never before had the cancellation of an engagement filled her with such fury. She had initially persisted in believing that Lord Arthur had not meant a word of it. All those previous jiltings had not even dented her superb vanity. But when she had returned to the hotel to find her father gleefully poring over plans for the new stables, she knew the engagement was definitely off. She had promptly sent a message to Mr. Palfrey, summoning him back, and had said she would help him in every way she could.

Mr. Barchester had grumbled most horribly over the amount of money it was taking to send his daughter to see the Queen. For he had had to pay a hefty bribe to get her invited and then there was the horrible cost of the court gown. He decided Lord Arthur should be made to pay for this extra expense. Besides, his daughter appeared to have a new beau in the shape of that fussy little man, Palfrey. Palfrey owned Tregarthan Castle. Mr. Barchester began to dream about an ornamental lake.

*   *   *

Miss Chubb cried with relief when Lord Arthur and Felicity returned to announce their engagement. Only Dolph was startled and disappointed to find that Brasnia did not exist.

178

All the long day they had waited for the return of the couple while Miss Chubb had told Dolph long and fanciful stories about the bears of Brasnia, feeling it politic to expand on Lord Arthur's strange lies. Dolph felt cheated. Brasnia had sounded like a marvelous place, and he had more or less made up his mind to go there.

So there was one last hurdle, the Queen's drawing room, and then they could all settle down to plan Felicity's wedding and discuss the future of their servants.

Lord Arthur left the next day with Dolph. Felicity passed her remaining days in Brighton in a daze of happiness. She almost forgot that Mr. Palfrey was probably still in London.

But once she was back in Chesterfield Gardens, the full terror of meeting the Queen drove everything else, apart from Lord Arthur, out of her mind.

Dressing for the occasion took hours of work. The minimum amount of large feathers allowed on the headdress was seven. Carberry's, the plumassier, had sent round twenty-four, deeming that the correct amount for royalty, but Felicity refused to wear so many and settled at last for ten standing up from a garland of roses resting on a circlet of white pearls. The mixture of jewels, flowers, and feathers required for court dress seemed odd to Felicity, who was used to wearing the simple Grecian fashions of the Regency.

She was strapped into a tight bodice, and then an enormous hooped skirt, three ells long, was laced to her waist. The skirt was made of waxed calico stretched upon whalebone, which made it very wide in the front and behind, and very narrow at the sides. Over that went a satin skirt, and over that, a skirt of tulle, ornamented with a large furbelow of silver lace. Another shorter skirt, also of tulle, with silver spangles ornamented by a garland of flowers, went on top of all that and was tucked up at the hem, the opening of each tuck being ornamented with silver lace and surmounted with a large bouquet of flowers. Then a lady attending court was also expected to wear as many jewels as possible. Felicity had the Channing diamonds as well as the pearls about her neck, her headdress was finished at the back with a diamond comb, and diamond buckles were attached to her shoes.

Miss Chubb, also attired in court dress, was so huge that she had to turn sideways to shuffle out through the front door. Two carriages had been hired to take them to Buckingham House, for their enormous skirts would not allow them to travel together. So Felicity had no one to talk to as she waited and waited in the long line of carriages that crawled toward Buckingham House.

At last she and Miss Chubb entered the great hall of the Queen's residence. A double staircase rose up to the drawing room above.

Those waiting to be presented went up by the left-hand staircase, and those who had been presented descended on the right.

Above the chatter of voices came the booming of the guns firing a salute in St. James's Park outside. At first Felicity and Miss Chubb had eyes only for the splendor of the display. Feathers of all colors were worn on headdresses. Jewels flashed and blazed. Ladies fidgeted and fretted, trying to protect their enormous gowns from getting crushed, and gentlemen in knee breeches and evening coats fiddled nervously with their dress swords.

As she began to ascend the staircase, Felicity sensed a malignant presence behind her. She wanted to turn around, but the great hoop of her gown prevented her from doing so. Then a familiar, tall figure ahead of her on the staircase turned and smiled, and she felt a great flood of delight and relief. For it was Lord Arthur, very grand in a dark blue silk coat and knee breeches. His black hair was powdered, and he carried a bicorne under his arm. His delight in the beauty of Felicity's appearance stopped him from noticing Mr. Palfrey and Miss Barchester close behind her.

All Felicity's fears left her. The masquerade was nearly over. One curtsey to the Queen among so many, and then she would be free to marry Lord Arthur.

By the time she and Miss Chubb had ascended the staircase, inch by inch, both were heartily tired of the long wait. And when it came their turn to be introduced, neither felt any nervousness at all as they sank down into low curtseys before Queen Charlotte, who surveyed them with great indifference and helped herself to a pinch of snuff.

Felicity was just backing away from the royal presence when a voice behind her cried, 'Impostor!'

One look at the so-called Miss Chubiski had been enough to convince Mr. Palfrey.

There was a hushed silence.

Then Mr. Palfrey said, 'Your Royal Majesty, my lords, my ladies, and gentlemen. This is not the Princess Felicity of Brasnia. This is Felicity Channing, my stepdaughter, who stole my jewels and ran away.'

Miss Barchester laughed. 'She is nothing but a paper princess,' she said.

A paper princess! A great hissing and whispering set the feathers nodding and dipping. Queen Charlotte looked at the stricken Felicity with mild curiosity. Then she raised her hand. Two Yeomen of the Guard stepped from behind her throne.

Lord Arthur came to stand beside Felicity and held her hand firmly in his own.

'This is indeed Felicity Channing,' he said, 'who is to be my wife. Your Royal Highness, let me tell you her story.'

'Better let me tell it,' said a portly man, waddling forward. 'I am Mr. Guy Clough, tobacco planter. I carry on me the late Mrs. Palfrey's last will, which this man'—he pointed at Mr. Palfrey—'tried to destroy.'

'Pray go on,' said the Queen. 'We have become interested.'

There were screams and yells from the staircase outside, where the guests who had not yet gained the drawing room, but who had begun to hear garbled whispers of an attempted assassination by a Turk, were beginning to push and shove.

So Mr. Clough told Bessie's story and handed the will to Felicity.

As everyone pressed forward to look over Felicity's shoulder, Mr. Palfrey backed away. The down staircase outside was empty; no one wanted to leave until they had learned every bit of the drama. He darted down it and disappeared into the night.

'Quite like a gothic romance,' sighed one sentimental lady. Ushers moved in to keep the guests in line. But Miss Barchester stood where she was, unable to believe the turn of events in Felicity's favor.

Queen Charlotte looked across at Miss Barchester, and her little monkey face creased in a frown. 'That woman,' she said. 'Have her removed.'

'It was nothing to do with me,' said Miss Barchester, turning white.

'You are only wearing six feathers,' said the little Queen. 'It is an insult to us. We suggest you do not aspire to social circles until you learn to dress.'

Despite her bewilderment and distress, Felicity could find it in her heart to be sorry for the ex-fiancée of Lord Arthur.

Tears of humiliation were running down Miss Barchester's cheeks as she made her way down the grand staircase.

'Let us go,' said Lord Arthur in Felicity's ear.

Clutching her mother's will, Felicity let him escort her down the stairs, past the goggling guests, who were still demanding to know if anyone had seen this murdering Turk.

*   *   *

At his hotel, Mr. Palfrey packed feverishly. He knew that the minute the initial shock of all the revelations had died down, a warrant would be out for his arrest. He was bending over his largest trunk, stuffing in shirts and small-clothes, when he heard the door behind him swing open. His heart gave a jump. But when he turned around, it was only Miss Barchester standing there, still in her court dress and with the despised six feathers, standing up on her head.

'You have ruined me,' said Miss Barchester.

'It was you who had the silly idea of challenging her in the middle of the Queen's drawing room,' pointed out Mr. Palfrey acidly.

'You had better leave, or they might arrest you as well.'

'I am ashamed. I shall never dare show my face in polite circles again,' said Miss Barchester. 'I shall go with you.'

'Charmed, dear lady,' said Mr. Palfrey, still packing. 'But may I point out that I have only enough money on me to take me out of the country. What I shall do when I get to the Low Countries to survive is beyond me.'

'Marry me,' said Miss Barchester, 'and Papa will give you my dowry.'

'How much?'

'Five thousand pounds.'

'Nearly enough, but not quite.'

'You still hold the Channing estates. Go to the bank in the morning and draw out as much as you can.'

'But the banker will have learned of all the fuss from the newspapers.'

'Then, you must trust to the fact that men of business rarely have time to read their newspapers first thing in the morning. I shall go with you. Perhaps this Channing creature will not want any more fuss and scandal and will not prosecute. So, do not draw out all the money, only enough to keep us comfortably.'

'I must leave this hotel immediately. Where shall I stay the night?'

'With my parents.'

'They will think it most odd.'

'Not them,' said Miss Barchester bitterly,

thinking that her father would only see Mr. Palfrey as a further extension to his estate. 'Come, I shall help you pack.'

There was something about Miss Barchester's stern, cold face that reminded Mr. Palfrey of his mother. With a weak little smile, he moved over and let her help him.

CHAPTER TEN

Felicity was roused early the next morning by Spinks, the butler.

'An urgent message from Lord Arthur Bessamy,' he said sonorously. 'We are to bar the door, close the shutters, and lock the windows.'

'Good heavens! What has happened? Has Napoleon invaded?'

'Vengeance is mine, sayeth the lord.'

'Pull yourself together, Spinks. Did not my lord explain the reason for his warning?'

'No, Your Royal Highness. But the end is nigh.'

'Don't be silly. Rouse Miss Chubb immediately, and bring me the morning papers.'

'I do not think that is a very good idea.'

'Do as you are told, Spinks,' said Felicity sharply. 'And you may now address me as Miss Channing. The masquerade is over.'

'Everything is over,' said Spinks in a hollow voice.

The minute he had left, Felicity jumped from her bed and made a hasty toilet. Miss Chubb came in just as Felicity was finishing dressing.

'What is all this?' asked the governess. 'Has Spinks gone mad?'

'Something awful is about to happen or Lord Arthur would not have sent a message.'

There came a scratching at the door, and the tutor, Mr. Silver, came in, carrying the morning papers and with an expression on his face as gloomy as that of the butler.

'Is it war?' asked Felicity nervously. 'Have the French come?'

'Worse than that,' said the tutor. He silently handed Felicity the newspapers and told her to look at the social columns.

Each paper carried a full account of the Queen's drawing room, and each damned this upstart, Felicity Channing, who had dared to masquerade as a royal princess and play a trick on 'our beloved Queen Charlotte.' There was not a word of Mr. Palfrey's perfidy. Tricking her out of her inheritance and nearly murdering a maid was small beer in the eyes of the press compared to Felicity's audacity in tricking London society. 'We had long noted,' said the *Morning Post*, 'a sad want of any royal traits in this paper princess.'

PAPER PRINCESS screamed all the other

journals. Miss Barchester had had her revenge after all.

'He will not want to marry me after this disgrace,' whispered Felicity. 'Lord Arthur's father, the duke, is very powerful and will stop the marriage.'

'Listen!' said Mr. Silver. There were howls and cries outside, growing closer.

They sat staring at one another. Soon an angry mob was below the windows.

'You wouldn't think they would be able to read the newspapers,' said Felicity.

'They don't need to,' said Mr. Silver. A stone rattled against the shutters. 'I am afraid, dear lady, that lampoons of you will be in all the print shops by now. The speed of the satirical artists of Grub Street never fails to amaze me.'

More stones began to strike the house and the roaring outside grew louder.

'If Lord Arthur guessed this was about to happen,' said Mr. Silver impatiently, 'then he should have arranged to protect us.'

'Listen!' said Miss Chubb. 'Someone is shouting something.'

Despite anguished cries from Miss Chubb to be careful, Felicity opened the shutters and looked down.

Lord Arthur Bessamy stood facing the mob. He was making a speech. They listened to him in silence, and then a great roar went up.

'Come away from the window,' shouted

Miss Chubb. 'They have seen you.'

'No,' said Felicity slowly. 'Lord Arthur is below. He made a speech, they all listened and cheered, and now they are going away as quietly as lambs.'

She turned from the window and ran out of the room and down the stairs to where John Tremayne was stationed by the door, holding a shotgun.

'Open the door,' cried Felicity. 'It is Lord Arthur.'

John drew back the bolts and bars and opened the door. Felicity flew into Lord Arthur's arms, crying, 'They are calling me the paper princess. Your father, the duke, he will never let you marry me.'

'Don't clutch my cravat,' said Lord Arthur amiably. 'Quite spoils the shape. My dearest, by next week they will all have forgotten you exist.'

'How did you get rid of them?'

'I told them about Palfrey. I told them I was going to marry you. But I think it was when I told them that I had arranged for free beer at the pub in Shepherd Market, for them to drink to your health, that started them cheering.'

'I was so afraid you would not want to marry me.'

'Idiot. But remember: It is to be our wedding, and only ours.'

'I do understand.'

'Miss Chubb and Mr. Silver may marry

when they please, but not at the same time as us.'

Felicity laughed. 'Poor Miss Chubb. Of course she is not going to marry Mr. Silver.'

'I fear you are blind to love,' said Lord Arthur. 'Why do you think Mr. Silver was so angry with poor Dolph? Now, do you want that wretch, Palfrey, arrested? After I left you last night, I went to call on Mr. Clough. He told me that Bessie is quite reformed and never wants to leave America.'

'No, I would rather let all the scandal die down.'

'Do you know the name of the bank where the Channing money is lodged?'

'It is Coutts in the Strand, I believe.'

'Then, I had better go there directly or Palfrey will flee the country with all the Channing money.'

He bowed and left, and Felicity went back upstairs to look at Miss Chubb and Mr. Silver with new eyes.

Lord Arthur was too late. He could only be glad that Mr. Palfrey had only drawn out ten thousand pounds. The estates, properly managed, would soon recover the loss.

CHAPTER ELEVEN

The Duke of Pentshire's home, Pent House, was a palace in the middle of rich green countryside. Felicity felt she had been hurtled down there out of the chaos of London and then left stranded with a great number of chilly people who did not approve of her one little bit. The duke and duchess, Lord Arthur's parents, were a handsome, formal couple whose exquisite manners barely concealed the wish that their youngest son had chosen someone else for a bride.

*　　　*　　　*

The couple were to be married in the private chapel. Felicity had made no suggestions of her own as to preparations for the wedding. There had been so much to do. John Tremayne had been parceled off to Lord Arthur's home to study estate management under the tuition of the steward. Dolph had volunteered to travel to Tregarthan Castle right after the wedding to take charge until such time as Lord Arthur could manage to join him and decide what was necessary to bring the Channing estates into good order.

Felicity's servants had either been pensioned off or found other jobs, according

191

to their wishes. Dolph had taken a fancy to Spinks, who he claimed was an original, and had said he would take the biblical butler with him as a sort of aide when he went to Cornwall. Mr. Silver and Miss Chubb were to be married and were to live at Tregarthan Castle until a home of their own could be found for them.

Contrary to Lord Arthur's hopes, society had not forgotten or forgiven the paper princess, and news of her masquerade had reached the august ears of Lord Arthur's father. Felicity had not been present during the long family arguments in which Lord Arthur's parents had tried to talk their son out of marrying her. But she felt their disapproval keenly.

There could be no reassuring hugs and kisses from Lord Arthur. If he took her out on the grounds for a walk, a footman was always in attendance, as the duke and duchess held strictly to the rules of society, which decreed that no couple should be left alone for a minute until after they were married.

Lord Arthur was beginning to become furious with his parents. He had been left a fortune by a distant relative and was economically independent of them, so they could not forbid the marriage, much as they wanted to. But he could not help feeling they might have put a better face on things.

If he had brought home some actress, they

could not have been more shocked.

The arrival of Felicity's sisters and their husbands did more to remove her from him, because she took refuge in her family's company in the guest wing, keeping as far away from his parents' aloof disapproval as she possibly could.

Felicity was feeling the strain even more than he guessed. In the stern lines of his face she began to read that he had begun to share his parents' distaste. Miss Barchester had seemed an odd sort of female for him to have ever proposed to. She could only be glad the duke and duchess had never met Miss Barchester. Her cold looks and old-fashioned dress would probably have pleased them. Felicity overheard the duchess saying one day with regret in her voice that it was a pity Arthur's previous engagement had come to nothing, for the Barchesters were a very old family. So were the Channings, the duchess had admitted, but Cornish! One never knew what went on in those castles and mansions down there, but it was well-known the Cornish were strange.

More of Lord Arthur's relatives continued to arrive, and the long formal dinners were an agony for Felicity. Miss Chubb was too wrapped up in her newfound happiness to be of much help. Lord Arthur, never allowed to sit next to her, was looking grimmer each day, and when Felicity retired with her ladies, she and her sisters were isolated in a corner of the drawing room as if they had the plague.

They were to spend their honeymoon in Brighton, Felicity having formed an affection for the place. While still in London, Felicity had looked forward to the honeymoon. Now she wondered if she would find she was tied for life to a man who bitterly regretted having proposed to her. It began to cross her mind that she might do him a great favor by running away. But to do so would spoil not only Miss Chubb and Mr. Silver's future, but John Tremayne's as well, who was so delighted and excited at the prospect of his new and important career. And then there was poor old Spinks. If she ran away, Dolph would have to drop the idea of taking Spinks to Tregarthan Castle, and Spinks had seen in Dolph's adoption of him the gracious hand of a benign God.

There was also all the great machinery of a ducal wedding that had been put into action. All tenants had been invited to a grand party on the grounds. Everyone appeared to have bought new clothes especially for the occasion. And if she ran away, the duke and the duchess would have the satisfaction of telling their youngest son that that was just the sort of disgraceful behavior he might have expected from an adventuress and impostor like Felicity Channing.

So her wedding morn finally arrived. She

was dressed in white silk and pearls while the rain fell steadily on the formal gardens outside and ran down the panes of the windows like fat tears.

How she was beginning to hate jewelry—hate the cold feel of pearls and the clumsy weight of diamonds. How she loathed the long corset that for some mad reason she was supposed to wear. It was so long and tight, she could only take tiny little steps. How she hated the cold, slippery feel of her white silk petticoat.

It was a gloomy, depressed couple who finally made their vows to one another in the family chapel. It was a grim silent couple who sat side by side at the wedding breakfast and listened to the interminable speeches. Dolph, elated with wine, and blissfully unaware of the prevailing chilly atmosphere, made a speech about how he had actually believed there was a country called Brasnia, told them about the bears, hiccupped and laughed immoderately, toasted the 'happy' bride and groom, and then sat down, heartily pleased with himself, not knowing that everyone who might have begun to forget about Princess Felicity of Brasnia was now remembering the disgraceful masquerade all over again.

Then Felicity was led upstairs to be changed into her carriage clothes. She looked desperately at Miss Chubb, dying to cry out for help, but that lady was smiling all over her large face and saying she was sure Felicity must be the happiest lady in the land.

Felicity's sisters hugged her and begged her to call on them when the honeymoon was over. Her clothes had been chosen for her by the duchess. A fussy carriage dress of brown velvet was put on over that constricting corset. The carriage gown was fussily tucked and gored and flounced. It was topped up by a navy straw bonnet shaped like a coal scuttle.

Lord Arthur was waiting inside the carriage when she made her way out. Felicity hugged her sisters, hugged Miss Chubb, and hugged Dolph, who was still laughing drunkenly about the bears, climbed in the carriage, and sat down primly on the seat beside her husband.

The carriage moved off.

Silence.

The rain drummed on the carriage roof, and the wheels whizzed through the puddles on the drive.

'Well, that's that,' said Lord Arthur at last.

Felicity said nothing.

'Do you know,' said her husband, 'I think you are wearing quite the most horrible hat I have ever seen.'

Felicity tore it off, threw it on the floor of the carriage, drummed her heels on it and burst into tears.

'Here now . . . now.' He pulled her into his arms. 'What's all this? Tears on our wedding day.'

'Oh, it's awful . . . awful,' sobbed Felicity. 'Your parents hate me, you hate me . . .'

'I don't hate you, you stupid little wretch,' he said crossly. 'I love you to distraction. I've had to watch your gloomy face and torture myself wondering if you no longer loved me and yet at the same time being frightened to ask you.'

'Oh, Arthur,' Felicity dried her eyes. 'I have been worrying about exactly the same thing.'

'We are both fools. Come and kiss me.'

He crushed her against him, and Felicity let out a yelp of pain.

'What is the matter?'

'It's this corset,' wailed Felicity. 'It has the bones of a whole whale in it, that I'll swear. I am laced so tight, I feel faint.'

Lord Arthur released her and jerked down the blinds. 'Take it off,' he said.

'What!'

'I said, take the damned thing off. We are married. We can do what we like. No relatives, no parents. I have not felt so free since I came into my inheritance and left Pent House to set up my own establishment in town. Take it off.'

Felicity giggled. 'You had best help me with your mother's choice of dress. Her maid lashed the tapes so tightly I think she had instructions to make sure I kept it on for life.'

'More than likely.' He dealt with the tapes expertly and began to slide the dress from her shoulders.

'You do that as if you were accustomed to it,' said Felicity sharply.

'I was always good at untying knots,' he said blandly. 'Goodness, what a monster that corset is. You'll need to lie on your face on this seat.'

Felicity lay down on her face while he struggled with the lacing of her corset, which had been lashed into a double knot at the back. Then he turned her gently over and began to unlace it at the front.

'Oh, what a relief,' sighed Felicity as he at last slid the corset from under her and chucked it on the seat opposite.

'Felicity,' he said hoarsely, looking down at the slim figure in the white silk petticoat.

'Arthur! You can't do anything yet. Not here! Not now!'

But his mouth silenced her, and his clever hands sent the rest of the world spinning away.

*   *   *

They were to spend the night at a posting house a comfortable distance away from Pent House.

Two tall footman jumped down and helped milord and milady to alight. The coachman and outriders took the horses and grand ducal carriage round to the stables.

'See if they've left anything in the carriage,' called the coachman to one of the grooms. 'Ladies are always leaving fans and reticules.'

The groom poked his head in the carriage and then reached in an arm. He then slowly backed out and mutely held up the corset.

'Well, my stars,' said the coachman, filled with admiration. 'Couldn't even wait. Ah, well, that's the Quality for you!'

*   *   *

Felicity awoke during the night with a frightened cry, and her husband hugged her close.

'I had a nightmare,' said Felicity. 'I dreamt I was back at Tregarthan Castle, and Mr. Palfrey was having me whipped.'

'Shhh. He cannot trouble you any longer. He has fled the country. I told you, Mr. Barchester said he had gone off and taken Martha with him.'

'It seems unfair that such a wicked man should go unpunished.'

'He's got Martha Barchester with him, and that is a fate worse than transportation. Besides, he will have to live in exile for the rest of his days. But now you are awake, I may as well take up where I left off . . .'

We hope you have enjoyed this Large Print book. Other Chivers Press or G.K. Hall & Co. Large Print books are available at your library or directly from the publishers.

For more information about current and forthcoming titles, please call or write, without obligation, to:

Chivers Press Limited
Windsor Bridge Road
Bath BA2 3AX
England
Tel. (01225) 335336

OR

Thorndike Press
295 Kennedy Memorial Drive
Waterville
Maine 04901
USA

All our Large Print titles are designed for easy reading, and all our books are made to last.